The BIG GOOSE and the LITTLE WHITE DUCK

by

MEINDERT De JONG

Pictures by Nancy Ekholm Burkert

HARPER & ROW, Publishers, New York, Evanston, and London

for
May G. Quigley

Contents

1

The Duck Who Was Forgotten

IT WAS this way. There was the little poultry store with the big glass window on the busy street. There were the busy people passing up and down, looking, as they went, into that big clear window. They would see all the cages with chickens and all the cages with turkeys. But they would not stop for that—they could see all that as they walked past.

But they did stop.

They would stop and say, "Oh, look at that big goose walking around the store!"

There he was, a great big gray goose with a very white downy breast. He walked all around the store. Sometimes he would walk to the back room. Sometimes he would walk right up to the window and look at the people standing there. He walked just wherever he pleased.

Then the people standing there would look still closer and say, "Oh, look at that funny little duck with a white tuft on his head following that big goose."

Under the counter the big goose would go. Under the counter went the little white duck. Around the cages the big goose would go. Around the cages went the little white duck.

The big goose never looked at all those busy, noisy chickens in the cages. But sometimes the little duck would stop, cock his head, and with one bright bead of an eye peer up at those chickens. But never for very long. Oh, no! By that time he would always have to hurry off after the big goose again.

"Now look how worried that funny little duck is," the people outside on the street would say. "He's afraid he won't catch up."

"Listen to him quack," they would say, and point their fingers at the little duck's yellow bill that opened and shut, opened and shut all the time he was hurrying after the big goose.

And that was where the big people in front of the store were wrong. They couldn't hear that little duck quack—not through that heavy plate-glass window.

But they couldn't even have heard him if they had gone into the store! That little duck had lost his voice. All he could say was: "Quack, quack, quack," in a tiny whisper. You could see he was saying quack, but you could not hear him—it looked for all the world as if he were talking to himself.

That was just the way it was at twelve o'clock of the day before Thanksgiving Day.

Now exactly at noon a big boy opened the door of the little poultry store. He was carrying a big case of chickens, and on top of that a high yellow bucket full of eggs. He was so loaded down he never saw the big goose. He almost stumbled over him and fell. He had just caught his bucket of eggs and saved it from falling and splattering eggs all over the store when the little duck got under his feet. And this time the tall yellow bucket of eggs came even closer to falling. But the big boy saved it—just in the nick of time, with not a half-second to spare.

The boy looked very cross. "Why don't you keep all your billy goats where they belong?" he said to the storekeeper.

"Billy goats? Oh, you mean my pet goose."

"Your pet goose? He almost broke my neck."

"And my pet duck."

"Your pet duck? It's a wonder I can still stand on both my legs."

"Well, you see I let them run loose because they are pets. And they're always together because they are pals."

"Your pals, maybe, not mine. Here, count those eggs and look at those chickens I brought. I want to get out of here before anything worse happens to me."

The big boy couldn't have been so very cross because when the storekeeper started to laugh, he laughed too. And all the time the storekeeper counted the eggs, the boy just stood and looked at the goose. He became so interested in that goose he quite forgot to watch the storekeeper count the eggs. Maybe the storekeeper counted ten too many—maybe he counted twelve too few. The boy would never know—he thought of nothing but that goose.

"How much do you want for that goose?" he asked at last.

"I have some nice fat chickens and turkeys," the storekeeper said. "Wouldn't you like a nice fat chicken? I think the goose is pretty old and tough."

The big boy laughed. "You're a funny man," he said. "Now why should I buy a chicken from you, when I've just sold you some chickens of my own. It's the goose I want."

"But don't you see—tomorrow is Thanksgiving Day," the man said in a sad voice.

The big boy frowned. "Tomorrow is Thanksgiving Day? Oh, yes, you're quite right," he said, and nodded his head very wisely. "And did you know that the next day would be the day after Thanksgiving Day?"

Then they both laughed.

"Oh, but you don't understand," the storekeeper said. "The goose is a pet, and I won't sell him for somebody's Thanksgiving Day dinner."

"But I didn't want him for somebody's Thanksgiving Day dinner. I wanted him for somebody's birthday. For a pet. To keep on our farm."

"Oh!" said the storekeeper. "Oh!" Then he was suddenly very happy and excited. "You catch him," he said over and over again. "You catch the goose. I'll sell him to you for a pet. I'll sell him to you."

"You see," the big boy tried to tell him, "today is my mother's birthday. She always wanted a big goose for a pet."

But the storekeeper did not hear him at all. He was too excited. "Let's catch him and weigh him up. Catch him and weigh him up," he kept saying over and over again.

He had not heard a single word that big boy had said.

"But what is the matter with you now?" the big boy said. He stood and stared very curiously at the store-keeper. "Why are you so excited?"

"But don't you see? He was my pet, and you don't know how worried I was that somebody would come in and want him for his Thanksgiving Day dinner. And then I'd have to sell him."

"But I promise I'll keep him on my farm as long as he lives," the big boy said.

That made the storekeeper very happy.

They both started out on tiptoe to circle around the goose. First the man took a step forward from the right side. Then the big boy took a step forward from the left side. Step by step they tiptoed closer to the goose.

"This is going to be some job—to catch that goose," the big boy said.

But it wasn't hard at all. The goose didn't even make one motion to get away. He seemed to like the big boy. He just let himself be picked up. And then he sat there quietly in the big boy's arms, looking up at the boy with his blue eyes. He looked the boy's face over—every bit of it. He looked at his nose and into his eyes. Then he reached up and nibbled the big boy's ear very gently. And then, as if it were a good joke, that goose chuckled deep down in his soft throat.

He just had to nibble that ear once more. And then he suddenly stretched his long neck way up and pushed his heavy bill through the boy's hair. He mussed it all up.

And all this time the little white duck stood on the big boy's toes, whispering his worried little quacks. Reaching up as high as he could. He was quite frantic. He just had to get up there with the big goose.

Nobody noticed him. The big boy didn't. The storekeeper didn't. Now if only he could have said "Quack, quack" very loudly. But he couldn't. So he was forgotten.

Why that man and that boy were so happy they forgot other things besides the little white duck. The big boy forgot to pay the storekeeper for the goose he had bought. The storekeeper forgot to tell him. They forgot about the crate the boy had brought the chickens in. And about the yellow bucket the boy had brought the eggs in.

With the goose under his arm the big boy just walked out of the store.

The little white duck waddled behind him, terribly worried and terribly excited. But the store door closed, and slammed in his face. No one noticed that little duck —not even the storekeeper.

And no one can tell what might have happened if a tall old man had not come into the store just after the big boy had left.

2

The Grandfather and the Goose

THE tall old man opened the store door. He never noticed the little duck—he just shoved him aside with the door. Then he closed it without ever giving that little duck a chance to get around the door and run down the sidewalk after the big boy with the big goose.

No, the old man never saw the duck. He just stood by the door and looked hard at the storekeeper.

"Isn't there a big boy here who brought a crate with chickens and a yellow bucket full of eggs?" he asked in a thin, hoarse voice.

"No, he was here, but he's gone," said the storekeeper.

"Gone? Where did he go? Can you tell me that? He had no business going. I didn't tell him he could go. I told him to wait here for me. I told him, 'You wait here while I get my hair cut.'"

The tall old man grew angrier and angrier as he talked. And the angrier he became, the faster he talked, and the faster he talked, the thinner his old voice became.

The storekeeper had to smile. "It sounds like you told that big boy a lot of things."

"Well, why shouldn't I? Can you tell me that? Why shouldn't I? After all, I'm his grandfather. He's a rascal, that's what he is—a rascal of a grandson."

The storekeeper shook his head. "No, he isn't," he said. "He's a nice boy. He even bought my pet goose. And just think—he didn't want that goose for Thanksgiving Day."

"Then what did he buy him for? Can you tell me that? He had no business buying a goose without first asking me. What did he buy him for?"

"He bought him for a present, I heard him say. A present for somebody's birthday."

"For my birthday?"

"I think so," said the storekeeper, but he wasn't listening to the old man. He was staring hard at the yellow egg bucket.

"Fine, fine!" the grandfather shouted. "So the big boy bought him for my birthday. For my eighty-eighth birthday. Well, isn't that nice! Then he isn't a rascal, after all. Think of it—roast goose for my eighty-eighth birthday. Are you sure he bought him for my birthday?"

"I guess so," said the storekeeper, but he wasn't listening to the old man. He was staring hard at the empty chicken crate.

"Fine, fine!" shouted the grandfather. "I've had everything—just everything—in my long life. All but goose. And now I'm going to have roast goose on my eighty-eighth birthday."

But the storekeeper had not heard a word the grand-father said. He was looking from the yellow egg bucket to the empty chicken crate—and from the empty chicken crate to the yellow egg bucket.

"Oh, oh, this is bad!" the storekeeper said to himself. "Oh, oh!"

"What are you oh-ohing about?" the old grandfather grumbled. "Why don't you listen to an old man when he's talking to you?"

"But don't you see? That big boy left his crate. He left his yellow egg bucket. And he ran off without paying me for my goose."

"He did? He did that? Well, then, why are you standing there? Can you tell me that? Why don't you run after him? I'm sure if I had young legs like you . . ."

The grandfather had no time to finish. He hardly had time to jump out of the way. The storekeeper ran by him. He threw the door wide open and ran down the street after the big boy.

He left the door wide open. That gave the little white duck his chance. Far down the street walked the boy with the big goose. After him ran the storekeeper, waving his arms and twirling his apron. And after him waddled the little white duck, his mouth wide open. Hurrying, hurrying, hurrying, without even time to say "Quack, quack."

Even the old grandfather came out of the store. But he did not follow the storekeeper. He just paced up and down in front of the store. Up and down, up and down, very impatient to see that fat goose.

"Oh, boy!" he would say. "Roast goose on my eighty-eighth birthday. Oh, boy!"

And every time he said "Oh, boy," he would take a little half-jump on his long old legs. And every time he finished saying it, he licked his lips—so anxious was he for roast goose.

But the big boy walked on. The storekeeper ran on. And the little duck waddled on. Far down the street.

At last the big boy heard the storekeeper's shouts. He turned and started to run back. The storekeeper turned and ran back. Only the little duck kept waddling on— slower and slower, for by this time he was getting very tired.

The storekeeper rushed right past the little duck

without ever seeing him. By this time the little duck was so tired he had to sit down right where he was. In the middle of the sidewalk.

The big boy was almost up to him now. One more step and he would have stepped right over the little duck without ever seeing him.

But the big goose had seen him. He had missed his little friend. He had been very puzzled to be carried off this way without the little duck. Never before in all their lives had they been separated.

And such a shout as that goose set up. He stretched his long neck and shouted and shouted. He pushed his big bill under the boy's cap—he pushed it right off. The boy stopped in his tracks. He looked at the goose.

"Now, what's wrong?" the big boy asked the goose. "I need that cap."

He stooped to pick up his cap. And then he saw. There right under his feet was the little duck. Happy now as he had never been before, but for all that just too tired to get to his feet.

And that is how the big boy came back into the store.

With a big goose under one arm and a little white duck under the other arm. All the people who saw it just stopped and laughed.

The storekeeper was surprised to see the little duck. But the grandfather only looked at the big fat goose.

"I forgot all about the little duck," the storekeeper said. "But you'll have to buy him, too. You see what he did. They just can't be separated. They never have been—they're pals."

The big boy shook his head. He set the little duck down. He hesitated. Then he set the big goose down, too. "Then I'm afraid I can't buy them," he said sadly. "I won't have enough money."

"How much is the goose?" the grandfather asked.

"Let me see," said the storekeeper. "He weighs sixteen pounds; that will be exactly one dollar and a half."

"Oh, boy! Sixteen pounds!" the grandfather mumbled softly to himself. "Sixteen pounds! What a birthday dinner that will be for me!" And he licked his lips.

"And how much for the duck?" the big boy asked. He looked so anxiously at the storekeeper he never heard what his grandfather was mumbling.

"The duck is fifty cents. That makes two dollars," said the storekeeper.

The big boy did not look anxious any more; he only looked sad. "Then I can't buy them," he said. "Then they will just have to go for somebody's Thanksgiving Day dinner. You see I still have to buy all the groceries for the farm."

Then the storekeeper looked sad, too. Even the grandfather started to look sad, but before he could quite get to looking sad, he became very fierce and angry.

"Do you mean you won't buy that goose?" he shouted at the big boy.

"I can't. Unless . . . unless . . ."

"Unless what? Don't you stand there unlessing me," the grandfather shouted.

"Unless . . . Well, would you be willing to go without sugar a whole week so I can buy the goose? If I don't buy sugar, and I don't buy pancake flour, and I don't . . ."

"Of course I would," the grandfather interrupted

him. "Of course I would. We'll make up for it on my birthday."

"On your birthday?" the big boy asked. He did not understand what his grandfather was talking about.

"Sure, on my eighty-eighth birthday."

"And meat. Do you think you could go without meat for a whole week so I can buy the goose?"

"Of course I could," the grandfather shouted. "Of course I could. I'll get plenty of it on my birthday." And then he chuckled deep down in his dry old throat.

The big boy looked at him. "On your birthday?"

"Sure, on my eighty-eighth birthday."

The big boy did not know what to make of it. But he saw his grandfather smile. And he heard his grandfather chuckle. It made him so happy that his grandfather was so willing to help him buy the goose that he smiled himself, and he laughed himself—a very long time.

The storekeeper laughed, too. But then he asked, "And now will you have enough to pay for the goose and the duck?"

The big boy figured it all over in his mind.

"No," he said. "I still won't have enough. Unless ... unless ..."

"Unless what?" the grandfather shouted. "Out with it. Don't you dare stand there unlessing me again."

"Unless you're willing to eat potatoes for breakfast." The big boy said it very softly. He hardly dared suggest such a thing to his grandfather.

"And what for dinner?"

"More potatoes."

"And what for supper?"

"Still more potatoes."

Then the grandfather was silent a long time. He looked at the big boy. He looked at the storekeeper. Last of all he looked at the big, fat goose.

Then he shouted. "Why, of course I will! Of course I will! That goose is worth it. And we'll make up for it on my eighty-eighth birthday."

"Then that settles it," said the big boy with a happy sigh. "Potatoes it is. Potatoes for breakfast, potatoes for dinner, and still more potatoes for supper."

"Now you should have enough to pay for the goose

and the little white duck," said the storekeeper very eagerly.

The big boy stood still. He figured it all over in his mind once more. Then he bit his lip. He became very, very still.

"No," he said in a very small whisper. "I still won't have enough. That poor goose and that poor little duck will, after all, have to be eaten on somebody's Thanksgiving Day dinner."

It was such a small whisper the grandfather and the storekeeper could barely hear it. It was almost as small a whisper as the little duck made.

The big boy did not say another word. He did not look at the storekeeper. He did not look at the grandfather. Without saying one other word, without looking at anyone, he picked up his crate and he picked up his egg bucket, and he started to march out of that store.

Then that grandfather became very angry. "Stop!" he shouted at the top of his hoarse old voice. "You stop where you are, this minute. Don't you dare run off without me again. I'll help you pay for that goose."

The big boy stopped, surprised. "What will you pay it with?"

"With my dollar. With my very last dollar."

"But why didn't you say you had a dollar? Here I figured and figured and figured."

"But it's my last dollar."

"But you know my mother will pay it back to you as soon as we get home."

"She will?"

"Of course she will. You know she will. If she has a dollar."

"And until then the goose is mine?"

"Until we get home and Mother pays you back, the goose is yours."

Then the grandfather chuckled. Then he fumbled in all his vest pockets until he found his dollar. He paid the storekeeper his dollar. Then the big boy paid the storekeeper his dollar.

"Let's hurry," the grandfather said. "You carry the crate and the bucket. I'll carry the duck and *my* goose."

And he walked so fast on his long old legs out of that store, the big boy almost had to trot to keep up with him.

3

The Goose Comes to the Farm

AFTER the big boy had left the store, he followed his grandfather far down the street to his little truck. There they carefully put the goose and the duck into the empty chicken crate. Then they put the crate in the back of the truck.

There wasn't much room in the back of that little truck. The big boy and his grandfather had to balance one end of the crate very carefully on top of three bags filled with feed for the cows and the other end on the tall, ten-gallon milk can.

That way the goose and the duck sat very high. Much higher than the cab of the truck. But after all that there was no room left for the yellow egg bucket. At last the big boy just hooked the bucket on behind the truck—where it banged and shivered and rattled.

The goose and the duck became very excited. They weren't a bit afraid to be up so high. They loved it. That way they could see everything. All the bright stores, all the fast cars, all the people walking down the busy streets.

Why it wasn't even high enough to satisfy the goose. He had to get still higher. He pushed his head through the slats at the top of the crate. Then his long neck. And he stretched that long neck as high as he could. And that was the way they rode through the town.

And that was the way—after the big boy had bought his few groceries—they rode into the country. Into the green country the goose loved.

The town was left behind. This was the country with its great trees, its green fields, and its long black plowed fields. This was the country the goose loved.

How fast the little truck was going now. Faster and faster, up and down the steep hills. The little duck was all out of breath; he acted almost as if he were running that fast himself. He even looked tired.

Oh, but that road was getting rough. There went the yellow egg bucket flying, bumpety-bump down a hill. A horse in a pasture, seeing that flying pail, lifted his tail and his two hind legs in the air all at the same time and tore down the pasture, snorting as he ran.

But at last, after one more hill, and after one more bend in the road, the truck slowed down. Then it turned down a long cinder driveway that led to a tall white house under tall pine trees.

The moment the big goose saw that farm he loved it. Every bit of it. The white house and the pine trees. The three sharp chimneys, very red and very sharp above the roof. The windows that blinked in the sun. The big red barn. The little white chicken coop. And even the tumbledown shed that was no color at all. The big goose wasn't quite sure yet—but he thought he loved that old shed best of all.

The big boy stopped the truck and jumped out. He

dashed to the door.

"Mother, come quick!" he shouted. "Guess what I've got for you."

His mother came as fast as she could. But she couldn't wait to guess. "Just tell me," she said. "Just tell me. I can't guess."

"A great big goose," the big boy said.

"A big goose? I always wanted a big goose."

"And a little white duck with a funny woolly tuft on top of his head—he belongs with the goose."

The big boy hurried to take down the crate from the truck. "It's for you," he said. "It's a birthday present for you—from Grandpa and me."

"A birthday present for me?" The boy's mother could hardly believe her ears.

But when the grandfather heard the big boy say that, he hastily scrambled out of the truck. He came with long steps toward the big boy.

"What's that you said, you rascal? What's that you're telling your mother?"

"I said it was our birthday present for her."

"For her? For me, you mean. For my eighty-eighth

birthday. Roast goose to eat on my eighty-eighth birthday."

"Eat the goose?" the big boy and his mother said, both at the same time. "Eat that goose? Why, he's a pet!" They looked at each other; they looked at the grandfather.

The mother looked at the big boy very sadly. "What is this, son?" she asked in a very soft voice. "For whose birthday is the goose, for Grandpa's or for mine?"

"Why, for yours. I never told Grandpa I had bought the goose for his birthday."

"Then it's all right. Then we will never eat the goose," she said very happily.

But the grandfather's face became very red. His eyes became very big. He became so angry he could hardly talk. He tried again and again, but all he could do was to make noises down in his throat. He swallowed and swallowed. At last he found his voice.

"You rascal!" he screamed. "You ungrateful rascal! The storekeeper told me you had bought the goose for my eighty-eighth birthday."

"But I never told the storekeeper that. I told him it was for Mother!" the big boy shouted.

"So you made me pay for a useless goose to keep on this farm. Made me pay my last dollar for a big, fat useless goose. A no-good goose that's going to eat all the corn for the chickens and do nothing for it. Why, you rascal! You, you rascal!"

"But, Father," the mother said, "maybe you misunderstood the storekeeper. Maybe . . ."

"Maybe nothing. Don't you maybe me! Who paid for the goose? Can you tell me that? Whose goose is it? Well, I'll tell you. Mine! It's my goose!"

"Oh, yes, Mother," the big boy said hastily. "Have you a dollar in the house? To pay Grandpa back. Grandpa helped buy the goose."

"Thank goodness, I have," his mother said. Without waiting another moment she flew to the house. When she came back, she had a dollar in her hand.

"Here, Father," she said. "Here is your dollar. And then the goose will be mine."

And then the grandfather chuckled. Chuckled and

chuckled deep down in his dry old throat. Very disagreeably.

"Oh, no." He laughed. "Oh, no. I don't want that dollar. You keep the dollar and I'll keep the goose. He'll be mine until my eighty-eighth birthday, and then we'll all have roast goose. Roast goose with pumpkin pie and cranberry sauce. Oh, boy!"

Then he suddenly turned. He strode off to the big red barn. "I'm going to find a good place for that goose," he called back over his shoulder. "A good place where I can lock him up and fatten him."

"But what about the little duck?" the boy's mother asked.

"Oh, that tiny duck. You can have him for a present. That's your birthday present from me." The grandfather chuckled.

"What will we do, Mother?" the big boy asked anxiously. "That big goose has never been locked up. He's never been away from the little duck. Shall I quickly take him back to the store where I bought him?"

"But if you take him back someone else will buy him

and eat him. No, we'd better keep him. Grandpa's birthday is still a long way off. Maybe he will learn to like the goose."

That was a fine thought. They both felt better after that thought.

"That's right," the boy said happily. "It will be months till Grandpa's birthday—anything can happen."

"Anything can happen," the mother agreed.

And now for the first time the big boy opened the crate and took out the goose and the little duck. The goose walked right up to the big boy's mother. And right away he loved her. Maybe it was because she had such a nice soft voice. Maybe it was because she was such a very tiny lady. Why, she had to stoop only a very little and the big goose could reach her face. She was so tiny.

Then that little lady stroked his fine soft chest. All the nice little feathers—she stroked them all smooth—they had become so ruffled from that wild ride. She even stroked the long stiff feathers of his back, and all the time she talked to the goose in her gentle voice.

The goose nibbled her shoes. He nibbled her shoestrings. He even nibbled her face very gently. And then it was all just too much for him. He spread his huge wings; he ran and he ran. He ran and he flew. Flew a little, ran a little, faster and faster. Past the windmill to the big red barn. Then back again, faster and faster, wings wider and wider. Faster, higher off the ground. Back to the little old lady—straight for her. Surely now he would knock her over, he was coming so straight and so fast. But he didn't, he didn't. He came straight, then just as he got up to her he sailed in a beautiful curve just around her. The tip of one wing just touched her dress. Then he stopped.

There he stood, very still, very proud, his huge wings still spread. There he stood proudly and looked up at the little old lady's face and into her eyes. Then he called and called, shouted and shouted. Louder, shriller, higher, and still higher.

The people on the next farm heard it. The old woman that lived all alone far down the road heard it. All the people in that countryside heard it. And they all wondered what it was. And nobody but the little old lady

knew that it was the big goose—the big goose in his own special way saying to the little old lady: "I love you, I love you, and I love you. And I will always take care of you."

The grandfather must have heard it too. For now he came running out of the big red barn. He was carrying a short piece of chain.

"Does that thing always make so much noise?" he asked.

"No, I don't think so," the little old lady said hastily.

"Well, he won't shout very long, because I found a fine place for him. In the big red barn. In front of the cow manger. It's nice and warm there. I'll tie this piece of chain around his leg so he won't get away. Then I'll just fatten and fatten him."

"But geese can't stand warm places," the big boy said.

"No, and this one can't stand being locked up. He's never been locked up before," the little old lady added.

"He'll just pine away," the big boy said.

"He'll get so thin he'll just be skin and bones," the

little old lady said. "And who wants to eat just skin and bones at a birthday dinner—especially at an eighty-eighth birthday dinner."

The grandfather looked at the big boy. "Is that right?" he asked.

He looked at the little old lady. "Are you sure of that?" he asked.

They both nodded their heads.

The grandfather looked at the goose. He looked at his chain. "Well, then, maybe I'd just better let him run loose in the big red barn."

"But why not let him run where he wants to?" the little old lady suggested.

"NO! Not if he shouts like that. Not if he makes that much noise. He's too noisy. Into the barn he goes. Right now. Right this minute."

"But, Grandpa, your coffee is ready. Surely you want your coffee first?"

"My coffee? Of course I want my coffee. You know that. Did you think I would bother with that useless goose before I had my coffee? But after I've had it—then

I'll put him in the big red barn."

The big boy looked at his mother. The little old lady looked at her son. They both smiled happily at each other. For they knew that they had saved that big goose from being kept on a chain.

4

The Goose Who Wanted
To Be Watchdog

NOW the little old lady had gone into the house. The big boy had gone in too, carrying all the groceries. Even the grandfather had gone into the house after he had put away the chain on which he wanted to tie the goose.

The little old lady had made a nice cup of steaming-hot cocoa for the big boy and a big mug of very strong coffee for the grandfather. A little later, after the big boy and his grandfather had milked all the cows, she would make their supper.

There were the big goose and the little white duck all by themselves in the big farmyard. The big goose wanted very much to see all the farm buildings—the big red barn, the little white chicken coop, and even the old tumbledown shed that had no color at all. He wanted to see just everything there was.

But did he set out with the little white duck to look at all those new buildings? He did not. The little old lady was in the house, and above everything else that big goose wanted to be near the little old lady. He had never loved anyone else so much. He looked wistfully at the old tumbledown shed. He listened wistfully to a cow mooing in the big red barn. But he sat down by the door the little old lady had gone through. He sat down on one side of the door. The little white duck sat down on the other side of the door. There they both sat and waited.

Maybe that little white duck was glad to sit down— he still was upset from that wild ride. He just had to be quiet for a little while and settle himself.

And just sitting there waiting by the side of the door, the big goose and the little white duck became acquainted with the farm animals. Without even having to move, without even having to stir. At least not at first.

First of all there came a little yellow baby cat. And did his eyes pop when he saw that big goose and that strange little duck sitting there beside the door! He wanted to get through that door.

There was a nice hole near the bottom of the door for the cats to go through. And behind that door, the little cat knew, was a saucer of warm milk for him. Oh, how badly he wanted to dip his chin in that lovely warm milk!

He sat down at a distance. First he looked at the little duck, and his eyes became quite round. Then he looked at the big goose, and his eyes almost became too round. He looked at that hole in the door between the duck and the goose. Behind that door was his saucer with milk. And then suddenly like a shot out of a box he dashed for that opening. One moment he was between the goose and the duck. The next moment, even before the goose could blink his eyes, the little cat's yellow bushy tail had disappeared through the hole. And behind the door the little cat sat, trembling and shaking. He couldn't even start to drink his milk without getting his whiskers all wet—he was shaking so. All for nothing—for neither that little duck nor that big goose had even made a move.

It must be feeding time for the cats, the goose thought. For hardly had the baby cat disappeared, when who should come sauntering to the door but a huge yellow-and-white cat. This was Oatmeal Joe. That is what the big boy called him because this big cat ate just as big a plateful of oatmeal every morning as the boy did. In fact, he ate twice as much oatmeal as the little old lady.

And here came Oatmeal Joe. He looked at the duck and at the big goose through half-closed eyes. Oatmeal Joe looked sleepy. In fact, he always looked sleepy; he never had his eyes wide open. He just looked once. He didn't go a bit faster, he didn't go a bit slower. He kept his own lazy pace. As he passed the goose and the duck he growled a little down in his throat, then he slowly squirmed his way through the hole in the door that was almost too small for him.

Right behind Oatmeal Joe came Tiby, the hunter cat.

He had long hair, slate gray. He was smaller than Oat-meal Joe, but he wasn't a bit more afraid. In fact, he wasn't afraid at all. He walked up to the little duck and sniffed very politely at the little duck's bill. Then he crossed over to the big goose and sniffed very politely at the big goose's bill. And the big goose nibbled his fur just a little bit. After that Tiby sat down right in front of the goose and licked his feet dry—they had become all wet from hunt-ing in the swamp. And after that he walked nicely to the hole—as much as to say: "We'll get better acquainted later, but first I must have my saucer of warm milk. I'm afraid it's getting cold."

That was the way the goose and the duck became ac-quainted with the three farm cats. Without even having to move or having to stir. But with Sam, the big shepherd dog, it was quite different. If it had not been for the big goose, it might very well have gone badly with the little white duck. As far as that goes, the little white duck came close to losing his funny woolly tuft. Even with the goose there.

In one way you couldn't blame Sam, the big shepherd

dog, for rushing at the little white duck. In a way it was almost his duty to grab first that little duck and then the big goose. Because Sam was the watchdog—he was supposed to guard the farm and the little old lady from all strange things. And both the goose and the little white duck were strange. Sam couldn't know they belonged.

But in another way the big shepherd dog was very much to blame. If he had not been out in the woods chasing rabbits when he was supposed to watch the farm and the little old lady, he would have seen the goose and the duck arrive. He would have seen the old lady and the big boy petting the goose and the duck. Then he would have known they belonged to the farm and were not to be attacked. But perhaps Sam felt just a bit guilty for going off into the woods and forgetting his duty. Perhaps that was why he was so fierce.

So before the big goose knew what was up, there Sam was, snarling and biting and barking. Almost before the goose could get to his feet, the dog had seized the little white duck, right by his woolly tuft.

But that was the last thing Sam did, for the next moment he found himself knocked over on his side. He was so surprised he let go of the little duck. He tried to turn to fight the goose. But he was just a little too late. Because the goose had already knocked him down and was standing right on top of him. With both his feet. He bit him here, bit him there. He tore out whole patches of the dog's shaggy hair.

That big dog was so surprised he gave up fighting right then and there. He didn't snarl any more, he didn't bite. He just squirmed and squirmed to get from under the big goose. When the goose noticed that he let Sam go, after once rapping him smartly over the head with his hard bill—just to be sure that Sam would remember never to touch the little white duck again.

There Sam, the big shepherd, sat on his haunches. His big eyes almost popped out, he was that surprised. His long tongue lolled out, he was that bewildered. And the little white duck stood tight against the goose and scolded and scolded that dog. Only nobody could hear him. But he was quite brave now after he had seen what the big goose could do, so he went right on scolding. For even if no one else could hear, it made the little duck feel quite brave inside.

It had been a very short fight. And it had not made Sam and the goose enemies at all. For now Sam knew that the goose and the duck belonged. But it did look as if that fight was going to change things on the farm.

It was just as if by that fight the goose had said: "From now on I'm the watchdog, and not you, Sam. I'm going to take care of the farm and my little old lady.

"You can go to the woods all day long and chase rabbits if you want to—you can never catch them anyway.

"I'll stay here in the farmyard.

"You can go chase sparrows in the pasture all you want—as if you ever could catch a sparrow.

"I'm staying here in the farmyard.

"You can go and dig in woodchuck holes till your tongue hangs out—as if you ever could dig as deep as a woodchuck.

"I'll stay here in the farmyard to take care of my little old lady.

"I'll shout when I see something strange.

"I'll fight anything that does not belong here.

"I'm not afraid of man or beast.

"I'm the watchdog.

"So you can chase rabbits and sparrows and wood-chucks all the day long. That is what you love best. You will be happy.

"I'll stay in the yard and take care of my little old lady all the day long. That is what I love best. I will be happy.

"I will be the watchdog."

Maybe it was lucky for that goose that he did not know the grandfather was going to lock him up. For how could he be watchdog locked up in the big red barn all the day long?

5

The Goose Who Was Punished

IT WAS right after the fight with the dog that the big boy came out of the house. The goose had just sat down again beside the door. The little white duck was hardly settled yet—he was still whispering to himself about Sam and the narrow escape he had had.

The big boy came out, eating an apple. He was carrying a milk pail. "Hi, goose! Hi, duck!" he said. But he did not stop. He walked straight to the barn to milk the cows.

The big goose got up when the boy came out. But he did not follow him. He sat down again. Then the little white duck sat down again too.

Next the grandfather came out. He was carrying three milk pails. He looked at the goose and frowned. Then the grandfather, too, walked straight to the barn.

But the big goose did not get up to follow him. Neither did the little duck get up.

And then after a little while the little old lady came out. Shall we take a walk, Goosie?" she asked.

That was the first time she had called that big goose Goosie. But ever after that she called him Goosie— maybe because he was so big—and Goosie sounded so small.

A walk was just what the big goose wanted. That was just what he had waited for all this time. Now he was going to see all the farm buildings and all the farm animals.

Toward the barn walked the little old lady. Close

behind her walked the big goose. And close behind the big goose waddled the little white duck.

The little old lady opened the door of the big red barn, and all three of them went in. First they came to a pen with two tiny calves. One all red, and one all white. How they frisked and danced around when they saw the goose and the duck! They dashed in little circles around their pen. They kicked their heels high. They jumped with all four feet off the ground at once—very stiff-legged and very wooden.

The big goose would have stood and looked at those two frisky calves a long time, but just then the little old lady turned around.

"Oh!" she said. "There's Prim. Prim has broken out of his pen."

Now Prim was the baby bull. The big boy had called him Prim because he looked so neat with his four little white feet. It looked just as though he wore white socks, for above those white socks of his all the rest of him was jet black.

That little bull came right for the goose. He was just

a baby bull. Why, he was hardly two inches higher than the frisky calves. But he thought he was quite a fellow.

He had been staked out in the yard during the summer, and from there he had watched the big black bull in the neighbor's pasture. The big bull was very ugly—he hated everything, even bushes and trees. He fought everything. The little baby bull had watched him very closely. Now he thought he knew just how to frighten that goose. He came for the goose just as he had seen the big black bull go for a dog, or a man, or even a tree.

"Oh, come quick!" the little old lady screamed. "Prim and the goose are going to fight."

The big boy came running. Then he just stood in the doorway and laughed.

On came the baby bull, rolling his eyes so that all you could see was the whites. Now he lowered his head just as he had seen the big bull do. He dug his little horns into the straw. He tossed his head, he tossed the straw. He bellowed and he snorted. Then he started to paw with his little front foot. He kept pawing straw and dust over his back. One little tuft of straw landed behind his horns

—it looked quite funny. He swept and swept his stumpy tail.

Then he stopped to look for the goose. Surely by this time the goose would have run far away! He peered through the dust and the straw he had raised. There stood the big goose. He had not moved an inch. He had not even shifted one feather.

The little bull didn't know what to make of it. Surely he had been terribly fierce. Now what to do? It was no use trying to be any fiercer. He looked at the straw and thought he would paw it some more. But then he changed his mind. And instead of being a fierce big black bull he became a little black calf with white feet again, as he really was.

He went up to the goose in a very friendly way. But not quite up to the goose, either. Just far enough so he could reach the goose with his long flat tongue. Then with his tongue he licked the goose—his whole neck and his head. The goose did not like it very much—but he seemed to know the little bull wanted to be friendly. But that tongue was rough. So rough it almost pulled out some of the feathers on the goose's neck.

So the goose, just to teach him not to be so rough, started to nip the little bull's ear. He didn't just nibble this time, he nipped, and quite sharply at that. And that little bull liked it! It seemed to feel good to him. And when the goose stopped, Prim would just put his ear very close to the goose as if to say, "Come on now, please nip it some more."

But although the big goose liked that funny baby bull very much, he couldn't stand there all day nipping his ear. So when the big boy put Prim back in his pen again, the little old lady and the goose and the duck went to look at the horses. In one stable was Molly, the sleek black horse. In the other was Topsy, the old white horse. The horses weren't excited as the calves had been. They went right on munching oats. They wouldn't stop eating even for anything as strange and new as the big goose. And most likely they never even saw the little white duck.

After this the little old lady took the goose and the duck to another part of the barn. There were the cows. A whole stableful. Chewing and munching away and making a great noise at their eating. When the cows saw the strange goose and the funny little duck, they breathed very hard. They looked so hard that their big round eyes almost popped out.

Then they went on chewing and munching again, chewing that sweet clover hay. And when they breathed hard, as they did when the goose walked in front of their manger, their breath was sweet from the clover hay. That whole barn was sweet from the clover-hay breath of those sleek cows.

There was a red cow and a brown one. Then there was one red and white. Next there were three black-and-white ones. And next to the last, toward the wall, was an all-black cow. But the cow next to the big black one, the one that stood against the wall, had little brown spots on her face—all around her nose. They looked for all the world like freckles—if you can imagine a cow with freckles.

And that freckled cow was the most inquisitive of them all. She quite forgot to eat. She stretched her head as far as she could toward the big goose. She even forgot that the grandfather was milking her.

That freckled cow stretched her neck so far she had to move her foot to keep her balance. And when she moved her foot she almost stepped on the grandfather's toe. But she was a very careful cow. She did not want to hurt the grandfather. It scared her so much she lifted her leg so fast and so high that she set it down again right in the milk pail.

That scared her even more. But it did not scare her nearly so much as the grandfather did. He shouted and bellowed at her. He called her names. There Grandpa made a terrible mistake. Because the cow was already so confused that she did not know what she was doing any more. She danced around. She jumped. She swished her tail. And the more she jumped, the louder Grandpa shouted. The louder Grandpa shouted, the worse that cow behaved. And there—she kicked. Kicked and kicked

And away went the milk pail. It smashed against the wall. All the milk spattered out, and the pail went banging over the floor.

And away went the milk stool. That cow kicked it right from under Grandpa.

And there went Grandpa sprawling. He landed on his back. Right under the big black cow.

It was a lucky thing for Grandpa that black cow was old and very sedate. She never moved a foot. She didn't even swish her tail. There lay Grandpa under the cow. His feet in the air. His red stocking cap in the straw.

At last Grandpa crawled from under the black cow. He got to his feet. First he was pale with fright, then he was red with anger, and then, when he saw the goose, he went purple with rage.

"Get that pesky thing out of here this minute!" he screamed at the little old lady. "This minute I tell you. And I won't even wait till my eighty-eighth birthday— next week I will eat him. That's all he's good for—to eat. He's no earthly use to anybody—he's nothing but a lot of trouble."

"But, Father—" the little old lady started to say.

But the grandfather would not listen. He waved his hands in the air. He stamped up and down the stable. He shouted at the top of his voice.

"And what's more," the grandfather shouted, "I don't want that goose in this barn. He scares the cows. Out to the old tumbledown shed with him. Hurry up. Right this minute—into the old shed."

The little old lady saw it was no use arguing with Grandpa. She hastily led the goose and the duck out of the stable. She almost ran because she saw the big boy was getting very angry.

"It wasn't the goose's fault," the big boy muttered. "It was Grandpa's fault—he shouted at the freckled cow."

Luckily the grandfather did not hear him.

There they went to the tumbledown shed—the goose and the duck and the little old lady. It was a pitiful old shed. Its roof humped here and sagged there, with a big hole in the middle through which the sky could easily be seen. Its walls were full of cracks and full of holes—there were even twelve boards missing out of the north wall. Its floor was ugly with dirt and rat holes and puddles. It did not even have one window. It had an old

door, but that hung on one hinge, and it had sagged so hard against the ground it could never be closed. Night and day, summer and winter, the door stood open.

And if the rain did not sweep through the open door, it swept through the north wall where the twelve boards were missing. And if the wind did not sweep and the rain did not hurl against the shed, the rain fell through the big hole in the roof through which the sky could easily be seen. It fell through the roof and it swept through the walls and it made the ugly floor one muddle of dirty puddles. All in all it was a horrible old shed.

And there the grandfather stood in the door of the cow stable. "Now I've really punished that goose." The grandfather chuckled. "How he will hate that shed!"

But what did that strange goose do? The strangest thing. He adopted that old tumbledown shed for his very own—for his bedroom—if you can imagine that!

Here, he decided, he and the little duck would sleep.

He did not mind the open door, he did not mind the missing boards. And he liked that hole in the roof. Through that hole in the roof he could see the stars at night. And through the holes in the wall he could see the morning come bright and clear to the farm he loved. And through that open door he could walk wherever he pleased. Over the whole farm. Over every little part of that farm he loved.

He did not mind the cold, either. He liked the cold. In fact, he would even have been quite happy to sleep outdoors—except perhaps in the very coldest nights of the winter.

But to be locked up in that big red barn that was warm from all the cows—that *would* have been punishment for the big goose.

And that goose decided another strange thing. From that first moment he decided that the little old lady would take him to the shed every evening, even though that old sagging door stood wide open, always stood open, and never could be closed.

This is what he decided: "Every evening when it's just late enough and just dark enough, I will call that little old lady in a very special way. And every evening the little old lady will come. She will take me to the shed.

She will say, 'Good night, Goosie; good night, little duck.'"

And the way the goose decided it, it happened. All but this very first evening.

For now the little old lady walked away without saying "Good night, Goosie." And without saying "Good night, little duck."

She was altogether too sad to remember to say good night. For she remembered what Grandpa had threatened.

"Next week," the grandfather had said, "next week I will eat that goose."

6

The Goose and the Runaway Pig

THIS was the week Grandpa had said he would eat the goose. In fact this was the last day of that week. And nothing had happened.

The goose had not been locked up as Grandpa had threatened. That goose had not been eaten as Grandpa had threatened. He still slept in the tumbledown shed, and he was still free to roam wherever he pleased.

First the little old lady had been very sad. She had hardly smiled at the goose. She had hardly talked to him. That little old lady had not been able to forget Grandpa's threat. It had kept her awake nights.

But now she smiled again. She even laughed again. She stroked the big goose's soft downy chest. And she talked to him in that nice soft voice she had. She took long walks with that goose.

"Surely," the little old lady had said to herself, "the grandfather has forgotten all about his threat. Or maybe he hasn't forgotten. Maybe he likes the goose and won't show it. Maybe he knows the goose is a good watchdog."

It was getting late in the season. It was late fall. Any day now and winter would be here. Some fine morning the goose would wake up and there it would be—winter would have come to the old farm.

The goose did not mind the coming of winter. He did not mind the cold. He did not even mind the crisp frosty mornings when smoke plumed out of all the chimneys above the roofs of the farmhouses. The people inside those houses might be cold, but not the goose. Not a bit. He took his bath every morning. Cold or no cold. In the dishpan behind the house he took his bath.

But every morning before he took his bath, he first walked to the house. Then he would trumpet loud and shrill as if to say: "Wake up, wake up—for surely it is morning. Wake up. Time to get up—for surely it is morning."

First a light would come on in the little old lady's bedroom window. She would raise her window, lean out and smile and say: "Good morning, Goosie. Good morning, little duck. You certainly are a useful alarm clock, Goosie."

Next a light would come on in the big boy's bedroom window. He would raise his window, lean out and grin and say: "Hi, there, you big alarm clock! Thanks for waking me up. I've lots of things to do today."

And last of all light would come on in the grandfather's window. He would jerk up his window, stick out his sleepy head, and scream: "Will you be still!"

After that terrible scream the goose would feel he needed a bath. He would immediately go to take his bath in the dishpan. That was the only way he could make himself feel better.

But this morning things were all wrong.

First of all, when the goose had gone to the house to give his morning call—nothing had happened. No light had come on in the little old lady's bedroom window. No light had come on in the big boy's bedroom window.

No light had even come on in the grandfather's bedroom window. But he had jerked out his sleepy head and screamed, "Will you be still!" Just that he'd said. Then he had slammed the window shut again. Harder than ever.

The goose felt terrible. It certainly was a terrible way to start the day. But if that only had been all. If that only had been all to make this morning a specially terrible morning.

He hurried to his dishpan to take his bath so he would feel better after Grandpa's scolding. But that went all wrong, too. There was ice on the dishpan. Thick ice. The goose had to strike it at last fifty times with his heavy bill before he could break the ice.

THE GOOSE AND THE RUNAWAY PIG 65

He felt a little better then. The water was icy cold, but he did not mind that. First he ran his head and neck way under the icy water, and then he would rub his wings, his chest, and every part of his body with his wet head and neck. He would dip his head in the pan again and again and then rub and rub.

The little white duck wasn't so white any more. The dishpan was too high for him to climb into. All there was left for him to do was to take a bath in the water the goose spilled. He really couldn't take much of a bath in those little puddles on the ground. It was more of a mud bath than anything else. But the duck didn't mind that at all. If there was anything he loved, it was dipping and dabbling around in little pools of muddy water.

This morning, though, the little duck was lucky. After all his rubbing and scrubbing the goose decided to take a real bath because this morning it did not make him feel any better just to wash himself in the usual way.

So he got into the dishpan. But he was too big for the dishpan. It is true he just fitted into it when he sat down. But that left no room for the water. So in went the goose

—out went the water. And the little duck had a glorious time splashing in the big mud puddles.

The goose did not know what to make of it. There he was in the pan—but where was the water? He dipped his neck and chest outside of the pan, but that only got him muddy. He was confused anyway this morning. Here he had called: "Wake up, wake up, for surely it is morning." Here he had been taking his bath a longer time than ever before and still the little old lady had not raised her window and called "Good morning, Goosie."

What was worse, the shade was already up. Come to think of it, that shade had been up when he first had come to the house. And the big boy's shade was up.

This worried the goose. He hurried to get out of the pan. But what did he do in clambering out but step on the edge of the dishpan. He tipped it over. The goose jumped. But the little duck had his head in the muddy water. He did not even see the pan coming. And it tipped over right on top of the little duck.

Such a scrambling and scratching as went on under the pan then. The goose did not know what to do. The little duck struggled and wrestled. He pushed his bill under the edge of the pan, but he wasn't strong enough to lift the pan. He tried again and again. It did not help a bit. At last he got tired.

It became very still under the dishpan.

The goose looked at the window; he looked at the door. He ran to the door and trumpeted very long. He ran to the window and trumpeted still longer.

Nothing happened. Only Grandpa came to his window. He shook his fist at the goose. He bellowed: "Stop that noise this minute."

He bellowed it right through the closed window. Then he disappeared again.

No old lady came. The big boy did not come. The farmhouse was all quiet again.

Then from the field the goose heard a shout. He looked, and there was the little old lady. Way back on the farm. And there, even farther back, was the big boy plowing with Molly and Topsy.

Then that goose was really puzzled. He must have overslept. Yes, that was what had happened. And here he had been calling: "Wake up, wake up, for surely it is morning."

And here the little old lady and the big boy had been up so long—they were already in the fields. The big goose felt ashamed of himself.

He had overslept. It was all the fault of that new little pig. The big boy had brought the new pig to the farm yesterday, just before dark. It was really Grandpa's pig— he had bought him, but the big boy had brought him to the farm.

That big boy had been so anxious to finish his plowing before winter set in, he had not even taken time to fix a pen for the pig. He had just pulled a big box into the old shed, put the little pig in, and put a window on top of the box. He had thrown a little straw into the box. And there it was—a big box now become a pigpen.

It was a cute little pig. Round and fat and pink. He really looked pink, although he had white hair. But the hair was so short and kinky that the pink skin showed right through.

But even though the little pig was clean and pink and cute, he had made himself an awful nuisance. At least, so the big goose thought. And the little duck had been quite excited over it, too, last night. He had quacked and quacked. For that tiny little pig, he was no bigger than a football, could make more noise than any one animal the goose had ever seen on that farm.

First the goose had decided to wait until the pig was quiet. But at last he had just gone into the shed. He had gone in mostly to please the little old lady.

But the cries of the little pig hurt his ears. The goose loved whistling. But what the little pig did wasn't whistling—it was just plain screeching.

It was very late before the little pig had gone to sleep. And so it was very late before the goose had gone to sleep.

You can see how the morning had started all wrong. There was the goose late. There was Grandpa in a terrible rage. There the goose had taken his bath in the mud instead of in the water. His nice white chest was all sticky and dirty. And there he had tipped the dishpan over on his little friend the duck. Luckily the little old lady was coming from the field. If only she would see that tipped-over dishpan.

The little old lady saw right away how muddy the

goose was. It was lucky she did, because then she looked at the dishpan. And when she picked it up, she was surprised to see the little duck pop from under it. And was the duck happy! He was so happy he bit her shoestrings. He was so happy he even let the little old lady pick him up. But that had never happened before, and he did not know how to behave nicely the way the goose did. Instead of sitting on her arms, he just let himself hang limp. There he hung, his head and neck straight down. You could see he was quite worried being up so high by himself without the big goose.

The little old lady petted the little duck, but she did not have a single kind word for the goose. And that had never happened before either. Then when he went up to her to be petted, too, she stepped back and scolded him. She turned away and filled the dishpan with water and then she went straight into the house. At the door she turned. "At least you had sense to call me after you trapped the poor little duck. But I almost think Grandpa is right. Sometimes you do seem a bit useless."

Then the little old lady turned very pale. She bit her lips. For there right behind her stood Grandpa. He had heard what she had said. And now he chuckled deep down in his dry old throat.

"Didn't I tell you?" he shouted. "Didn't I tell you he was useless? Now is there any reason to wait until my eighty-eighth birthday? Can you tell me that? Can you give me even one good reason?"

Now the old lady was really worried. She bit her lips, so vexed she was that she had given Grandpa an excuse for eating the goose. She chewed her lips very hard. For now she could not think of one reason to stop Grandpa from eating the goose.

And then she jerked her chin up. There—she'd thought of a very good reason. Her face brightened. She almost smiled.

"You'll just have to wait," she said. "You'll just have to wait till your eighty-eighth birthday. You see, I haven't any roasting pan that's big enough for that big goose."

"No roasting pan?" Grandpa screamed. "No roasting pan! Well, then, I'll get you a roasting pan right this minute. I'll walk to town and buy you a roasting pan big enough for any goose. I'll . . ."

Grandfather did not even wait to finish. He rushed through the house. He tore off his old red stocking cap and put on his black derby hat instead.

There he went—down the road on his tall old legs. He took great big steps. He swung his arms very hard. He lifted his feet very high. He was in the greatest hurry to get to town to buy a roasting pan in which to roast the big goose.

The little old lady hurried into the house. She could not bear to look at the big goose. She felt very sad. She felt it was all her fault.

The big goose felt sad too. The little old lady he loved had scolded him. She had gone into the house without even so much as looking at him.

The goose was angry himself. Not with the little old lady. He was angry with the new little pig. It was all that little pig's fault. If the little old lady had known that he had hardly slept all night she would not have scolded him so. That goose would have liked to bite that little pig. Bite him hard.

And then he looked up and there stood the little pig!

Outside the door of the shed! That was all wrong! He would run away. He would get lost. There he stood, sniffing with his nose up in the air. Sniffing toward the east, then toward the west. He held his nose very high and very still for just one moment. And away he went. Straight for the road.

Fast? How that baby pig could run! He looked for all the world like a pink football traveling with the speed of a bullet down the driveway to the road.

The goose jumped up and ran to the window where he knew the old lady was mending socks. How he shouted, how he screamed! At the top of his voice. Louder, then still louder.

The goose could see the big boy back in the field. He had stopped his horses and stood looking. But from there the big boy could not possibly see the little pig running down the road. And the little old lady did not seem to hear. She did not lift her head—she did not even try to look out of the window.

The goose became quite frantic. How was he to know that the little old lady had her head bent because

she was silently crying? How was he to know that little old lady did not dare to lift her head and look out of the window for fear she would see the grandfather come striding down the road with a great big roasting pan?

No, the big goose thought the little old lady was still angry with him.

And that made the big goose absolutely frantic. He opened his great wings. He flew right at that window. He shouted and screamed and beat his wings.

Oh, didn't that lady know that all this time the little pig was running and running? Farther and farther from home every minute. Didn't she know that if she waited just a little longer they would never get the little pig back?

But now at last the little old lady got up. She didn't look out of the window, but now she was walking to the door.

The goose ran to the door. Then as soon as the little old lady opened the door, he ran to the front yard.

Oh, why didn't that lady hurry! Why did she just stand by the door—she could never see the little running pig from that back door. Why didn't she step out into the yard? But the little old lady wasn't in a bit of a hurry. She still thought the big goose was only coaxing her to come out and pet him.

But she also knew by this time that the big goose set up a clamor when anything was wrong. She looked all around. And then she saw! There was the little pig bowling along at great speed along the side of the road. Straight as an arrow he went along the neighbor's fence. She called to the big boy. "The pig is running away," she screamed at the top of her voice. The big boy must have heard her, for he started running across the field toward the road.

If the little pig could run, so could the big boy. In one jump he was over the fence and then on the road. Down the road he went after the little pig. As he ran he called to the hired man next door. Then he called to the farmer across the road. There they came running too.

It was the funniest sight seeing those three big men all running at top speed after that little bit of a pig. The pig was now getting near the big ditch that ran alongside the road. If he got in that ditch, he might go in the drain pipe that ran under the road. Then they would never get him out.

Ben, the hired man, came running with great big steps. His boots made a lot of noise on the gravel. The little pig saw him, turned around in one wink, and ran straight back exactly the same way he had come. At least he had been kept from going into the ditch and under the road. Now he ran straight for the big boy and the farmer from across the road.

First he came toward the farmer.

"Grab his tail," the big boy shouted.

"Grab his leg," the hired man yelled.

The farmer from across the road grabbed his little round football body instead. That was no use. There was nothing to hold on to anywhere. The little pig just went through his arms like water.

On he came. Faster than ever after that scare. On and on, faster and faster. Now it was the big boy's turn. He waited. He stood very still. The little pig in all his hurry never saw him.

The big boy waited until the little pig was just past him. Then he threw himself into the air, like a football tackle. Right on the little pig he landed. He grabbed him around the neck with both his hands, he pinned him against his chest with his arms.

What a screaming and screeching went up then. The little pig squirmed and wriggled. It was getting hard to hold him. He was biting and snapping at the big boy's hands. Luckily the other two men now came running up. They helped the big boy. At last the big boy got up from the ground, carrying the pig.

Together the boy and the little lady and the goose and the duck brought the little pig back in his box. They put a heavy stone on the window, and there he was all snug and safe again. That little pig was so tired he fell sound asleep the minute he was in the box.

And the goose was petted then! His soft, downy breast was stroked. He even had a ride on the big boy's head. And the little old lady carried him in her arms. And she whispered in his ear: "I'll never call you useless again!"

She was so happy she forgot all about the grandfather. Then she looked up—and there came Grandpa striding up the driveway. He had a big blue roasting pan under one arm. He had hurried so that all the paper had come off and was fluttering from one corner of the pan. All the string had come off and was wrapped around one of Grandpa's legs.

The little old lady hardly dared look at that roasting pan. It was the biggest she had ever seen. It was almost big enough for two geese. It was surely big enough for both the big goose and the little white duck.

She hugged the goose tight in her arms, and she walked right up to the grandfather with him—she looked him right in the eyes.

"Now, when you hear what I have to tell you, you won't think this goose is useless. He saved your little pig," she called out.

Grandpa waved his one free hand. "You don't have to tell me a thing about it. Not a thing. I saw it all from the road. Every bit of it."

"And don't you think the goose is useful now?"

"Useful? Of course I think he is a *bit* useful." The grandfather looked at the big boy. "And what do you think? Can you tell me that? Do you think the goose is a bit useful?"

"Not a *bit* useful," the big boy said. "*Very* useful. He wakes me up early every morning. I've already finished all the fall plowing. I never had that finished so early before. He's a grand alarm clock."

"And a grand watchdog," the little old lady added. "He watches every single minute of the day. He's much better than Sam. And he saved your pig."

The grandfather hesitated a long time. He looked at his roasting pan. He looked at the goose. He listened to the little pig snoring in his box. He looked at his roasting pan again. Then he smiled a bit to himself. Then without another word he marched straight to the barn —the big blue roasting pan still under his arm.

He set it on a high shelf above the horse stables.

Molly, the black horse, and Topsy, the white horse, looked very queerly at that blue roasting pan when they came into the barn. The grandfather chuckled when he saw those horses look at the big pan out of the corners of their eyes.

"You'll have to get used to it, horses," he said and chuckled again. "That pan stays there. Maybe a long time. Maybe until my eighty-eighth birthday. Yes, I think I'd rather have roast goose on my eighty-eighth birthday—that's more appropriate."

The grandfather stood still a long time. He thought about it a very long time. Then he licked his lips. He could not help licking his lips when he thought of the grand eighty-eighth birthday he would have.

7

The Goose and the Pekin Ducklings

IT WAS spring now. Winter had not really been so very long. At least the big goose didn't think so now that it was spring.

Not now. Not with the grass green and tender again. With the cows chewing quietly in the pasture. With the big boy and the two horses far away over the ridge of the hill. With the old mother chickens all around the barnyard clucking and clucking to their broods of little yellow chicks. And with the hundred little Pekin ducklings in their brooder house.

There had been bad days in winter. Days when it was so cold the goose had to sit on his feet to keep them warm. Days when his water had frozen so solid that he couldn't take a drink and surely not a bath. Days when he did manage to take a bath, but the water turned to ice on his feathers. When every feather would have a little icicle on its end. When his neck would be stiff with ice, and when every time he moved, the ice in his feathers would make tiny rinkling, tinkling sounds.

There had been days so bitter that he dared not even come out of his old shed. Days when the wind howled and blew, when the wind whistled through the knot-holes, when the snow and the sleet hurled through the hole in the roof and through gaps in the walls. Days when the snow almost filled the open doorway of the old sagging door.

On those days the little old lady would clamber over the banks of snow and bring the goose food and water.

Several times a day she must bring him water because it froze almost as fast as she brought it.

Those had been the really bad days of winter.

But in another way the winter had not been so bad. Had not been bad at all. Because the goose was still free—Grandpa had not locked him up. And the goose was still alive—Grandpa had not even threatened to eat him.

In a way you would think that the grandfather almost liked the big goose. He did not growl any more when the goose woke him up in the morning. Every since the goose had saved the little pig, Grandpa had not growled at the big goose in the morning.

It is true he never picked up the big goose in his arms. He never talked in a special soft voice to the goose the way the little old lady always did—and the way the big boy sometimes did. He never stroked the goose's soft, downy chest.

But in a way you would think that Grandfather almost loved the big goose. Even the big boy thought so.

"Maybe," he said to his mother, "Grandpa won't eat

the goose on his eighty-eighth birthday after all."

"Maybe," she would say doubtfully. "Maybe." For she knew Grandpa. "Maybe if that goose should prove extra specially useful." And then she would sigh. She could think of no way of having that goose prove extra specially useful.

She could not forget that roasting pan on the high shelf in the stable. She could not forget that Grandpa's birthday came in late spring.

And here it was early spring. Birds sang and built nests. Grass grew thick; trees were getting leaves. The whole barnyard was alive with chickens, with cows coming and going to pasture, with horses coming through, pulling the creaking old wagon. But most of all, the best of all, there were the little white Pekin ducklings in their warm coop.

Those Pekin ducklings belonged to the grandfather and the big boy. The grandfather had bought them, but the big boy took care of them.

The goose often watched them through the window.

There they ran and dashed around the hot brooder stove. He could see the flame of the stove red and yellow on the window. He could hear the growl and hum of that big stove. And then to see those little ducklings eat! That was funny. They gulped their food in such huge mouthfuls that to get it down they had to stretch their necks straight in the air and shake and shake their whole little bodies— to get that food down. That whole flock of ducklings standing there in the hot room shaking as if they had the chills.

And how they grew! It was such a short time ago when they had been tiny. Four of them would hardly make a handful. Now suddenly there they were big, and then bigger. Growing, growing, growing. Eating, eating, eating. There never had been anything like those ducklings.

Today the big boy was moving them to the orchard. They were old enough and big enough now. They did not need the warm stove any more. When they were babies they had been yellow, but now their growing feathers had turned those ducklings white.

The big boy fed them more and more every day. It seemed as if they could never get enough. First it had been a pailful for the hundred, then it had been two pailfuls, and now it was already a wheelbarrowful. They would hear the squeek of the wheelbarrow far off. And what a racket then! What a quacking! Even the big goose could not shout above the noise.

The big boy shoveled the feed right out of the wheelbarrow onto the ground. Big shovelfuls. But hardly had the feed hit the ground, when it was gone. The ducklings didn't have to shake it down any more now; they just gulped and swallowed.

And after their feeding they would become very quiet. They would hardly move at all—just sit growing bigger and bigger. Soon they would be as big as the little white duck, then they would be bigger than the little white duck, and then in just a few weeks they would be full grown, big and fat and heavy.

The big boy had fenced off a small corner of the orchard for the ducks. When that was finished, he went to fetch the horses to drag a coop into the orchard where the ducks could sleep nights. The big boy worked so fast, he was in such a hurry, he quite forgot to close the gate of the duck yard.

The big boy hurried away; he never saw that open gate.

The little old lady was busy in the house, she never saw that open gate.

But the big goose saw the gate stand open, and he took up his post squarely in front of that open gate. Then the ducklings did not dare to come out of their yard.

The grandfather hurried by. He saw that goose standing there near the ducklings. But he never noticed that open gate.

"What are you doing there, goose?" the grandfather shouted. "You don't belong with those ducks. You see that you get in the front yard."

So the big goose had to walk straight to the front yard. He stood by himself in the driveway. He felt worried about those ducklings.

The big boy was in the barn. The little old lady was in the house. The grandfather was in the chicken coop.

Nobody saw the first white duck move toward the gate of the duck yard. Nobody heard him quack to the other ducks. There they came, all in a tight little group. They walked so close together there wasn't even a little bit of space between them. They were pressed so close you couldn't see their feet. All you could see was the white group moving, moving ahead. And you saw their dark little beads of eyes.

The ducklings knew what they wanted. They did not want to be locked up in a little corner of the orchard. They wanted to see all of the countryside. Their farm and the neighbor's farm and the long white road with the ditches on either side—full of water.

On they came. Past the chicken coop. Past their own brooder coop. Through the back yard and down the long driveway that led to the road. On they came. But there in the driveway, blocking their way, stood the big goose.

The first ducks stopped when they saw the goose; the ones behind marched on—right over the first ones. All of them scrambled over the first ones, until the first stood up again. But the very tail end ducklings were now the

leaders of that parade. And the first were last.

Now all of the ducks saw the big goose, and all of them moved away. All the hundred ducks moved as one duck. They wheeled around and headed toward the wheat field.

The big goose did his best to drive them back into their duck yard in the corner of the orchard. It was no use. The more he tried, the more those ducklings scrambled and fluttered and wheeled. He could not get them near that gate at all. Straight for the wheat field they went.

Behind the wheat field was a little pond, quite big now from all the spring rains. It was a weedy pond, and it had tall reeds all along the edges. And at one end of that pond was an old willow tree that had fallen over and started to grow again. It was a very pleasant pond—full of little frogs and full of little insects. The big goose and the little duck often went there to swim.

Perhaps the big goose thought the hundred white ducklings were going to the pond. Perhaps he thought it would be nice for them to have a swim, too—all the water they had ever had was a little in a dishpan. Any-way, he started to walk behind them, and with him came the little white duck.

It was far from the house. Even the little white duck got tired walking there. And these hundred white duck-lings were so fat, so heavy, they couldn't make the trip all at once. At times all hundred just sat down and rested. Then the big goose would stop too. And so would the little duck.

But now as they were getting farther and farther from home, with everything looking so strange, and that huge goose right behind them—the ducklings became afraid. They tried to turn around and go back home. But there was the big goose just walking back and forth be-hind them. He had to walk that way—these ducklings were so fat and so slow, if the big goose had walked straight ahead he would have passed all the ducklings. Why, he would have been in the pond and swimming long ago!

With the big goose walking back and forth that way, the ducklings saw no chance to turn back, so on they trudged, pressing close together. Getting more tired and more tired. Resting, walking, resting again.

But at last they did reach the pond. And when they stood on the bank and saw the quiet water in the shade of the old willow that hung over the pond—what a scramble then! They never remembered they were tired. They forgot all about how far they were from home. Into the water all of them went. All of them together, all diving at once.

It was beautiful. There was the quiet pond covered with white floating ducks. They floated here, they swam there. They dove, they poked their heads into the mud, they pulled and tugged at weeds. They chased each other under the hanging branches of the fallen willow tree. And right in the midst of them was the little white duck with his little white tuft. Faster than any of them, deeper than any of them, under longer than any of them he went. What fun they had.

And on the bank stood the big goose. He did not go in the water. He just stood and watched them all.

The big boy came back to the orchard. He looked

everywhere. He saw the open gate and rushed back to the brooder coop to see if the ducks had gone there. Not a single duck could be seen.

"Mother," he shouted, "Grandpa's ducklings are gone. Every last one of them."

The little old lady ran to the door. She too looked high and low. She looked down the road. She looked down the deep ditches alongside the road. She even looked in the neighbor's pasture. And the big boy poked his head into the doorway of the tumbledown shed. They just couldn't imagine what had become of the ducklings. They knew the ducklings were too slow to travel very far.

They did not dare tell the grandfather. They hoped he would stay in the chicken coop. But there he came. He looked at the big boy dashing about. He looked at the little old lady running from the back yard to the front yard and back again.

"Now what's wrong?" he shouted.

"The ducklings," the big boy said. "They're gone."

"I knew it. I knew it. Then you left the gate open! And that big goose drove them down the road. I saw him there at the gate of the duck yard. You're a rascal, and that useless goose . . . Wait till I get hold of him."

"But where *is* the big goose?" the little old lady asked.

They all listened. And there they heard the big goose's shout. It came quite faint—it seemed to come from the pond. "Maybe that's where the ducklings are," the little old lady told the big boy.

"Maybe," he said, and started running.

Grandpa ran after him as fast as his tall old legs could carry him.

Sure enough—there they all were. Happy? They had never been so happy in all their lives. The big boy watched them a long time—it was such a pretty sight. He kept watching them even while he was stroking the big goose and telling that goose what a fine fellow he was. He watched them until the grandfather came up.

Even the grandfather had to chuckle at that pretty sight. And even the grandfather started to stoop over to stroke the big goose's chest. But then he saw the big boy was looking. So he hastily straightened up. He hastily made believe he had been scratching his knee.

The big boy had to smile.

"You take care of them, Goosie," he quickly said. "And when they've had enough—you bring them back to the house again."

Then he turned and ran as fast as he could to tell his mother all about how Grandpa had almost stroked the goose.

"Don't you think he was extra specially useful?" the big boy asked. "Don't you think that now maybe Grandpa won't want him for his birthday dinner?"

"Maybe," the little old lady said. "Maybe." But she did not say it quite so doubtfully this time. And she did not sigh. She even smiled a bit. "Maybe," she said again, and she smiled again.

Now the goose stood at the edge of the pond, feeling very proud. Even after the big boy and the grandfather had left, that goose still stood there very proud. He puffed out his chest as far as he could. And he watched each one of those happy ducklings very carefully.

He was proud because the big boy approved of him.

He was even prouder because the grandfather had approved of him. He was too proud even to admit to himself that he would like very much to get into that blue water with all the white ducklings.

Perhaps if that big goose could have known what a big mistake he was soon to make, he would not have been quite so proud. It might even be that the goose was just a bit too proud right then!

8

The Goose Takes a Horseback Ride

THE goose made his big mistake for the strangest reason. A very strange reason. He made his mistake because he loved little girls. All little girls.

Of course, he loved the little old lady most of all.

Oh, he loved the big boy, too, but not with that special love he had for the little old lady. The grandfather he did not love at all—but that was not surprising.

No, if he had not loved that little old lady best of all,

and if he had not loved little girls so well, he might never have made his mistake. But there it was—he loved that little old lady. He loved her even better than he did the little duck. In fact, all he thought of was the little old lady. He spent his days just wandering around the house, listening so he would know in just what room she was working.

And if she did not come out soon enough to suit him, he would call and call to her. But if that also did not help, he would go to the dining-room window, and then he would rap and rap on that window with his bill so that it rattled.

The little old lady knew that when the goose did that, he was so impatient for her to come out and pet him—there was nothing for it but to go out there and talk to him, and stroke his soft downy throat, and pick him up and hug him.

Then that goose would be satisfied. Then he would be happy for a long time.

This day too the goose was very impatient for the little old lady. He had called and called, but she had not come. He wanted to rap on the dinning-room window —but he could not rap. He could not even get near that window.

It had all happened because of Grandpa. Yesterday when the goose had rapped on the window, it had been just when the grandfather was in the house. It had made the grandfather so angry for fear the goose would break the window that the little old lady had rushed right out to fix a little fence in front of the window—because she was afraid the grandfather would do something terrible to the big goose.

And now the goose wanted the little old lady, and he could not rap. And this happened to be one of the little lady's very busy days.

It was a very busy day. First of all the big boy had to go to town to deliver his eggs. She had to pack all the eggs. When the big boy delivered eggs, he also took butter along. She had to churn all the butter. And then when the big boy was finally on his way—there was all her house in a mess. All her housework still to be done. And four pairs of Grandpa's socks still to be mended.

The little old lady simply had no time for the goose. She heard him call, but she paid no attention.

It was such a lovely day, too. The sun shone against the dark green trees. The grass was almost blue, so green it was. And the whole road was white with light.

The goose was getting terribly tired of waiting for the little old lady. The morning was so long, so very, very long. It simply did not seem to wear away.

And here it was afternoon at last. Two little girls were coming down the road. One was dressed in green; the other was dressed in red. They were happy and gay. They laughed. Sometimes they even sang little songs.

The goose had seen them coming way in the distance. They were coming nearer and nearer. He became really excited then. He talked about it to the little duck. He shouted about it to the little duck. But that little duck was sleepy in the warm afternoon sun. He tucked his head farther and farther under his wing so he could not hear the goose. He could not understand why the big goose made all that fuss.

How could he know that goose loved little girls?

How could he know that goose became excited over the little girls' voices? They were nice voices—nice and soft and tinkly.

There the girls were in their beautiful party dresses. Now they were in front of the house. They were passing it. They were in a big hurry as they walked by, talking and chattering about the party to which they were going.

The goose did not know what to do. He looked at the duck. He looked at the house. He looked at the window. He looked at the door. If only the little old lady would come out—then he could tell her all about the beautiful little girls with the nice tinkly voices.

No one came. The door stayed shut. The house stayed quiet. Slowly, looking back again and again to see if the old lady really wasn't coming out of the house, the goose went down the driveway. The little duck waddled close behind him. At the road the duck stopped. The goose would have stopped, too, but just then the little girls burst out laughing. And it sounded so pretty to the big goose on that road white with light, he just left the duck behind and hurried after them.

Away the little girls went, hurrying for the party.

Away the big goose went—hurrying after the girls. And the little duck went back to the house, quacking sadly to himself in his tiny whisper.

The big boy came back from town. He drove his truck into the yard. There was the little white duck sitting all huddled and sad in a little bit of a white bunch at the door.

"Where's the big goose?" the boy asked the duck.

"Where's the big goose?" he asked his mother when she came to the door.

"I don't know," she said. "He was around the house all morning, just shouting at the top of his lungs. But come to think of it—I haven't heard him for quite a while now."

The big boy went to the red barn and looked all through it. He looked behind the chicken coop. He even looked in the tumbledown shed. Nowhere was there a sign of the goose.

He shouted to the grandfather back in the fields hoeing beans.

"Grandpa," he shouted at the top of his lungs, "did the big goose follow you to the field?"

"He did not," the grandfather screamed back. "What do you think? Think I want that goose back here pulling up all the bean plants?"

The little old lady sighed when she heard that. "Then where can he be?" she asked the big boy anxiously.

"I know," the big boy said. "I'll climb up in the windmill. From there I can see the whole countryside."

The big boy ran up the ladder. Higher and higher he climbed as fast as he could. And then still higher. He was above the tall maple tree, now, that grew near the windmill. He stopped a moment, but still he was not satisfied. He climbed still higher. Now he climbed onto the little platform under the big blades of the windmill. There he stood holding onto the tail of the windmill. There he stood looking first in this direction, then in that direction. First east, then west, then north, then south, then in all directions at once. Over the fields. Over the woods. Over the hills.

The wind blew off his cap; it landed on the roof of the chicken coop. The wind whipped his hair. It jerked at his shirt. His red necktie stood out straight.

Then all of a sudden he stood very still. He looked and looked. Down the white gravel road he saw a little girl in a green dress, another little girl in a red dress. And behind them—he could, yes, he could just see it bobbing. Could he be sure? Yes, he was sure now. Behind them he could just see the bobbing head of the big goose. He could just see his head and it bobbed and it bobbed—the big goose must be walking very fast.

The big boy scrambled down that windmill in such a hurry that his mother down below shut her eyes tight. She was afraid. She was almost sure he would fall, he was in such a hurry. She wanted to warn him, but her tongue was dry in her mouth. She couldn't say a word. She felt almost the way the little duck must have felt when he wanted to shout and could only utter a little whisper.

The big boy got down all right. But his face was pale.

"He's way down the road, following two girls," he shouted to his mother as he ran for his truck. "He's almost to the main cement road near the village. And if he crosses that road, he'll be killed."

Already the big boy was in the truck. He put his foot on the gas, but nothing happened. He tried again and again. Still nothing. At last he got so anxious and disgusted that he threw the keys against the chicken coop.

What to do now? The old truck wouldn't move, and all the time the big goose was getting closer and closer to the cement road.

The big boy knew how fast the cars whizzed down that cement road—just as fast as they could go. One car after the other—swoop it went, and it was gone. And then the next and the next and the next. The big boy knew, too, that the goose wasn't one bit afraid of cars. He wouldn't even try to get out of the way. And the cars went too fast to stop for anything.

The big boy fumed and fretted. He ran here and ran there. What to do! What to do! He almost started to run to the road, but it was no use trying to run. Why, it was almost a mile to the village. He could never get there fast enough.

Then he saw Molly, the black horse. She was right

by the gate of the pasture. Now he knew what to do. If only Molly would not run away clear to the other end of the pasture, as she sometimes did when she did not want to be caught. The big boy hastily climbed through the fence behind Molly. Molly saw him just a moment too late. She wheeled away and started to run. But the big boy already had hold of her neck and mane. As she ran he swung himself up.

Now how to open the gate was the big problem. But while the big boy was running after the horse, the little old lady had run to the gate. She was opening it. Right through the gate, away they went. Clippety-clop, faster and faster. To the road, down the road. Up the hill, down the hill, and over another hill. Away and away, faster, faster, faster.

Straight down that narrow road Molly went, straight as an arrow. She did not swerve to one side of the road where there was a deep ditch; she did not swerve to the other side where there was an even deeper ditch. On they went, down the second hill and on to the third hill.

But up that third hill they almost had to come to a

stop. They had to slow down to a crawl. The big boy bit his lips—he became desperate with impatience. But there was nothing he could do. A big truck was crawling up that third hill. It was so wide the horse could never pass that truck. There were the two ditches on either side of the road.

That big truck could hardly make the steep hill. It coughed and it spluttered. Oh, if it only stopped.

But it didn't stop. It didn't stop. It coughed and it spluttered but it crawled on slower and slower.

The big boy fumed and fretted. "Molly," he said. "Molly, we have to do better. We'll never get there in time to save the goose."

As if that horse could do any better than she was doing!

But it seemed Molly understood. Without any warning that horse swerved right for the side of the road. Straight for the deep ditch.

The big boy flattened himself. He stretched himself low over the stretched neck of the flying horse. He clung with all his might onto that horse's mane.

There they went. In one great leap. Up in the air and over the ditch. The big boy held on for all he was worth. He grabbed his hands deep into the mane. But for all that, his legs flew up in the air. For a moment he almost stood on his head—on the back of the horse. Then the horse landed with a thump on the other side of the ditch. The boy landed with a thump down on Molly's back. Away they went—along the fence. Along the truck and beyond the truck.

Then that horse jumped back on the road. Once more the boy almost stood on his head on the back of that horse. Once more he landed with a thump.

Then the big boy saw the goose and the girls. His heart went in his throat. The girls were standing on the edge of the cement road waiting for a chance to cross. A few feet behind them stood the goose. It did not look as if the girls knew the goose was behind them.

"Faster, Molly! Faster! Hurry up! Hurry, hurry, hurry!"

Molly stretched her long legs still more. The gravel spattered. The wind sang through the big boy's hair. He crouched low over the horse's head. If only the cars kept coming so those two girls couldn't start out across the road!

They were getting close now. "Hey!" the big boy shouted. "Hey, you two girls stand where you are!" But one of the girls had just taken a step into the road. For a moment the cars had stopped rushing by. The other little girl was all ready to dash across.

The girls turned and waited. They saw the goose. They saw the mad dash of the horse and the boy. The one in green screamed just a little, but the one in red wasn't afraid. She couldn't understand what it was all about. But she wasn't afraid.

The boy stopped the horse just a little behind the girls. Now the goose saw him, too. And did he shout!

"What's the matter?" the girl in red asked.

"Oh, our goose followed you. I saw him from our windmill. And I knew if I couldn't stop you before you crossed the cement road, he would get run over by a car. He won't move for cars."

"But now what are you going to do with him?" the girl in green asked.

There was a problem. The big boy couldn't walk and lead the horse because he had nothing to hold the horse with. He looked at his red necktie—but you couldn't pull a horse with a necktie. And the goose was very tired. Walking a whole mile was a long stretch for him. He would never be able to walk all the way back.

"Are you afraid of the goose?" the big boy asked.

"*I'm* not," the girl with the red dress answered.

"Would you dare lift him off the ground?"

But that was quite a thing to ask a little girl to do, lift up a big goose she had never seen before. Even the girl in red didn't like the idea one tiny bit.

"He won't hurt you," the big boy told her. "He likes you. That's why he followed you way out here. Just put your arm around him and lift him up."

The little girl hardly knew what to do. She walked toward the goose, reached out her arm, then drew it back quickly. "I'm afraid I don't quite dare take hold of him," she said.

"Look," the big boy said, "I'll reach way down and then you just quickly lift him. It's the only way." He clamped his legs around the horse and he reached way down as low as he could toward the ground.

"Pat his chest, and then you'll know he won't hurt you," he told the little girl.

Again the little girl in red was going to pick up the goose. But again she lost courage just at the last moment.

"Oh, we're going to be late for the party. Hurry and pick him up!" the little girl in green said.

"Well, why don't *you,* if you're so brave?" the little girl in red answered. "I don't see you trying to do anything."

"All right, I will. I'm not going to miss any more of that party than I have to."

And then the little girl in green, who had screamed at first, and who had been really afraid, picked up the big goose. The goose held himself very quiet. But he was heavy. It was quite a lift. But when the other little girl saw that, she helped lift, too, and together they got the goose just high enough so the big boy could scoop his arm under him and lift him up on the horse.

"Thank you very, very much," the big boy said. "Have a nice time at the party."

And there was the big goose on top of the horse. The big boy steadied him with his hands; and that was the way they went down the road. Molly did not run now. She just walked. She was tired. And anyway the goose could never have stayed on if she had run.

Was that goose proud? At every farmhouse he called out very loudly to all the people. He clucked and he chattered. He puffed out his white chest. Then when they got near home he grew so bold he even tried to climb on the big boy's head. The big boy had quite a struggle to keep him down.

"No, you're high enough," the big boy told him. "You just stay on the horse."

And that was how the big goose went horseback riding. And you should have heard him tell the old lady about it. He told and told, but he just simply couldn't tell enough about it. And every now and then he would get so excited, he would spread his big wings and run and fly as fast as he could to the windmill. Then run and fly back even faster. Right up to the little old lady.

He would stand on the toes of her shoes, stretch his

neck as far up to her face as he could, and then just tell and tell still more, still more. Louder and faster. At the top of his voice. Everything over and over again. And nobody scolded him. The little old lady and the big boy and the little white duck were altogether too happy to have him back again for anyone to want to scold him.

Even Grandpa did not scold him. He was busy in the tumbledown shed fixing a fattening-crate for the goose. He waited until the big boy was in the barn. He waited until the little old lady, who had gone to the pasture to give Molly the horse four lumps of sugar, was back in the house. Then he went to catch the goose.

He felt him all over. He felt the goose's legs, his chest, his back. Then he shook his head.

"This will never do," he grumbled. "If you're going to get spring fever and run away, I'll have to lock you up. You're running yourself thin. Maybe you don't even weigh as much as when I bought you."

He picked the goose up. He carried him to the scale. There he weighed him.

"Fourteen pounds," he grumbled when he read the

scale. "And when I bought you, you weighed sixteen pounds. This will never do. You're running yourself thin. You're as thin as a dime."

He carried the goose straight to the fattening-crate.

"In you go," he said. "Into the fattening-crate. Here it will be my eighty-eighth birthday very soon and you all the time getting thinner. What do you think? Do you think I want skin and bones for my birthday dinner?"

But he did not put the goose in the fattening-crate. He hesitated.

Maybe the grandfather remembered that the big boy had said the goose would pine away if he were locked up.

Maybe he remembered how that goose had saved his little pig and guarded his hundred ducklings.

Maybe he did not put the goose in the fattening-crate because in his own grumpy way Grandpa, too, loved the little old lady. He knew it would hurt her.

Anyway, he did not put the goose in the crate. He let him go. And that was very fine of Grandpa. In a way that was very nice. But in another way it was not so nice.

In a way you might say the goose almost deserved it for making his terrible mistake in running away. Certainly he had deserved it much more now than when he had proved himself very useful.

This was the sad thing about it. Grandpa did not put the goose in the fattening-crate when he deserved it. But he did put him in right after that goose proved himself most useful. Almost more useful than ever before.

9

The Rat in the House

THIS is how it happened.

The house was really too big for the little old lady and the big boy and Grandpa. They could not use nearly all the rooms. They used only one bedroom upstairs, and they used only two of the three bedrooms downstairs. Well, they did use the third one in a way. They used it as a storeroom. But really it wasn't a proper storeroom either, for you see, the house was so big and had so many nooks and crannies, so many cupboards and closets, there was room enough for almost anything.

There was nothing in this storeroom but some empty boxes, empty baskets, and useless clothes. Now under the window was a rather big hole in the brick foundation. The hole had come in that wall a long time ago. Almost a year ago. Long before the goose had come to the farm.

As soon as the big boy had seen the hole, he had gone to his grandfather. "Will you fix that hole?" he had asked. "Rats and mice and even squirrels can come into the house through that hole. And you know how afraid Mother is of rats."

"Certainly I will fix it," the grandfather had said. "I'll fix it proper. I'll mix some water and some cement and put it in the hole. No rat will ever get through that. I'll fix it proper."

Later in the day the little old lady had noticed that the hole had not yet been filled. She had gone straight to the grandfather.

"Will you please fix that hole, Father?" she had asked. "I'm afraid of rats."

"Certainly I'll fix it," the grandfather had said. "I'll mix some water and cement and I'll even put little stones in that cement. You needn't worry about rats. I'll fix it up proper."

Then he had gone to take a nap in the hay. He had forgotten all about that hole through which rats and mice and squirrels and all the little outdoor animals could come into the house. He had forgotten all about it until late that night. Then he had stolen out of the house and hastily stuck a bottle in that hole.

"Tomorrow I'll fix it up proper," he had said to himself.

But he had forgotten all about it. The little old lady and the big boy had forgotten about it too.

And there was the hole. And there was just that round bottle in the hole to stop mice and rats and squirrels from coming into the house.

Or, rather, there the bottle was not in the hole any more. It happened just as the big goose walked by the storeroom. That bottle fell out. It made quite a clatter.

The goose became very excited. He ran to the bottle. He stuck his bill into the hole under the storeroom window. This was all wrong! He did not know why the bottle had been in the hole. But he did know it belonged in the hole—not lying in the tall grass under the window. He set up a great clatter.

He shouted and screamed and scolded. He set up such a noise that the little old lady came running out of the house, the big boy came running out of the barn, and Grandpa came running out of the chicken coop.

They were puzzled. They couldn't find any reason for the big goose being so excited.

First they thought a strange dog was on the farm.

The goose kept right on shouting. He stood near the bottle and kept on shouting.

Then they thought there was a tramp in one of the buildings. They looked through all the buildings, but they could not find a thing.

The big goose put one foot on the bottle in the tall grass and went right on shouting.

The big boy walked over to the goose. The goose talked to him very fast. He tried and tried to tell him over and over again. The goose stopped. The boy was looking at the storeroom window. Surely now he would notice the hole under the window. Surely now he would see the bottle in the grass.

But no. The big boy looked here, looked there, but he never noticed anything. He patted the goose a few times to quiet him, but even then he did not see that bottle right under his nose.

Then Grandpa became very angry when he saw the boy pat the goose.

"There you stand and pat that thing," he screamed. "Some watchdog. Some wonderful watchdog. All that noise for nothing. There he stands and shouts and screams all about nothing."

The little old lady hastily went into the house. The big boy hurried back to his milking in the big barn. The grandfather went muttering into the chicken coop.

The goose felt so bad he did not even care when he saw a big black rat steal out of the chicken coop and make straight for that hole under the storeroom window.

Or rather, he pretended he did not care. It really made

him quite nervous and worried to think of that big black rat there in the house with his little old lady. But the goose did not dare to shout about it. He did not dare to warn anyone. So no one but the big goose knew there was a rat in the house.

No one knew until evening. The little lady and the big boy and the grandfather were having supper. Suddenly the little old lady sat up very straight—she listened hard. The big boy went right on eating—he was hungry, he had worked hard. Grandpa went right on eating.

The little old lady said sharply, "I hear a rat. He's in the house."

The big boy immediately stopped eating, but the grandfather kept right on.

The big boy listened a moment. Then he too went right on eating—he was so hungry.

But the old lady could not eat any more. She sat bolt upright. She listened and listened for more sounds.

"There, I hear him again," she said.

"Nonsense!" Grandpa grumbled. "Nonsense! How could a rat get in the house? And if there is—well, we'll just send that wonderful watchdog goose of yours after him."

The little old lady did not say anything more. But she looked very pleadingly at the big boy.

The big boy looked a little sadly at his plate. But he got up when he saw that anxious look on the little old lady's face. He took one hasty sip of milk, then he marched to the storeroom.

"All right, Mother," he said, "I'll take a look."

The big boy walked very softly into the storeroom. And he closed the door again very softly. But for all his soft closing of the door, he shut it very tight—he knew how afraid his mother was of rats.

He poked into the closet. Out jumped a rat. He jumped right past the big boy. Now that rat was in the storeroom. The big boy hastily slammed the closet door shut so the rat could not get back to the hole under the storeroom window.

The big boy looked all around for a weapon—there wasn't any weapon of any kind. Just boxes and baskets and useless old clothes.

At last he found a box with a few old worn-out slippers of his mother's. The little old lady wore such tiny slippers that really they weren't much good for chasing a rat. What was worse, they had soft soles and heels—they were really no good at all. But it was all the big boy could find in that storeroom.

He grinned a little to himself—it was funny chasing a rat with a tiny lady's slipper. Around and around they went. Sometimes the big boy ran, sometimes he crawled on hands and knees behind the rat. Once he just managed to slap the rat with the tip of the slipper. That rat just ran all the faster—that was all the good it did.

Then that big boy just sat down flat in the middle of that storeroom and laughed and laughed. Laughed and laughed.

"You'd think he was a horse that I had to whip because he was slow," he said to himself. And then he laughed some more. And you can't be very good at catching rats when your sides are just shaking with laughter.

All this time the little old lady had been standing outside the closed door. When she heard the big boy laugh, she thought he had caught the rat. And she was thinking what a brave son she had to go in there all by himself and catch a rat. But when the big boy told her why he was sitting there laughing, she thought he was even braver—just imagine sitting there laughing with a big black rat just a few feet from you. The little old lady shuddered to think of it.

"Maybe I had better bring you one of the cats," she said.

She went outdoors and called and called. The big boy could hear her. Higher and sharper her voice went. "Kitty, kitty, kitty, kitty." At last she came back. "It's funny," she said through the door, "but when you need them, they're always gone."

"Didn't a single one come?" the big boy asked.

"Oh, just the little yellow baby cat. I've got him here, but he's so small, he wouldn't be any good."

"Give him to me," the big boy said. "The rat is twice as big as he is, but maybe if the rat sees the cat, he won't watch me so closely and then maybe I can get him."

The little old lady opened the door just far enough

to push the little cat through, then she hastily slammed it shut again.

The little yellow baby cat saw the rat. He ran up to the rat. The rat saw the little cat. He had been desperately running and running round the room but now he stopped and let out a scream.

The little cat stopped dead in his tracks at that scream. He shivered a little. Slowly, very slowly, he backed up where the big boy was and he stayed right close to the big boy after that. When the big boy moved, the little cat moved too, very tight up against him.

"You're a big help," the big boy told the little cat. "Now I've got to take care of you and still catch the rat myself. But then you're such a baby yet—this is too much for you, isn't it?" And he stroked the little cat. And the little cat felt ever so much better then, not so afraid any more. But he still stayed as close to the big boy as he could.

"Is he too small?" the little old lady asked through the door. "Because I've got Oatmeal Joe here now. He came at last."

"Good," the big boy said. "Oatmeal Joe is big enough for any rat. With his six claws on one paw, he ought to be just the thing for this big rat."

In came Oatmeal Joe. Bang went the door again. In one big leap Joe was after the rat. Around boxes, between boxes, over baskets around and around they went. But the rat was faster than the cat. And the big boy became all excited. He raised his slipper high. There was the rat just a moment in the open. The big boy threw the slipper with all his might. But the rat was just out of the way, and there was Oatmeal Joe instead. And instead of the slipper hitting the rat, it hit Oatmeal Joe squarely on the head.

Oatmeal Joe stopped right there. He looked at the big boy and growled a little. He was insulted. The big boy laughed helplessly. "I couldn't help it, Joe," he explained. "I was trying my best to help you. Anyway, you needn't get so mad about it. It was only a soft slipper."

But the big boy could talk all he wanted, Oatmeal Joe was through. He sat right where the slipper had hit him and growled a little to himself.

The rat was terribly afraid now with that big cat in

the room and no escape anywhere. Even though the cat wasn't chasing him, he kept running round and round, squealing at the top of his voice. Sometimes, he was so blind with fear, he ran very close to Oatmeal Joe. Did that big cat stir—not Oatmeal Joe! He curled his big six-toed paws under his body and sat. He even blinked his eyes. It made the big boy angry.

"If you refuse to do anything, I don't suppose I can

make you," he told Oatmeal Joe. "But if you're going to sit there and go to sleep with a rat running almost over you, you're going to get another slipper on the head. Or maybe one of these big boxes.

"Oh, Mother," the big boy called then, "bring me Tiby—he's a hunter. He can handle the rat."

"I've called and called," the little old lady said, "but I suppose he's way back on the farm, hunting again. I'll try once more."

The big boy waited while his mother called Tiby. Then he heard a strange sound—like the sound of something hard dragging over the floor. The boy jerked the door open. Then he saw. It was Grandpa. Grandpa with the goose.

But that grandfather did not carry the goose the way the big boy carried him. And the way the little old lady always carried him. He did not carry him in his arms. He carried that big goose upside down—by his legs! That was what had made that dragging sound. The big goose was hanging head down and his hard bill was dragging over the floor.

Grandpa threw the big goose into the storeroom. "There," he said. "Maybe this wonderful watchdog goose can catch a rat. Now if he did that, I might really think he was quite some use."

The big goose was confused. He felt ashamed. Never in all his life had he been carried that way—upside down by his legs!

He slowly managed to scramble to his feet. Then he just stood in the middle of that room and shouted and scolded. He scolded the rat, he scolded the cats. He even scolded the big boy—he was so confused.

The grandfather had gone to finish his supper alone. But with all that shouting and all that scolding, he became so curious to see what that goose could do that he too came into the storeroom.

"Pipe down! Pipe down!" he shouted at the goose. "We know you can make plenty of noise. But noise doesn't catch a rat. Let's see you catch a rat."

And that goose did try. He was really angry now. He was angry with the grandfather for having carried him in that awful way. But he was furious with the rat.

He stretched out his long neck. His big red tongue came out. And how he hissed. Hissed and hissed. He almost sounded as if he were boiling over. How he hated that rat for coming into his little old lady's house.

He spread his great wings. He charged straight for the rat. Again and again. All around that room. He knocked over boxes, he ran into baskets, he got old clothes around his neck. But that was about all that happened.

But with all that noise, all that banging, and all that hissing the rat went almost mad with terror. He dashed around the room. He even tried to run up the walls. And if he had squealed before, now he squealed twice as much and twice as loud.

Everybody in the room was very much excited now. Everybody, that is, but Oatmeal Joe—he still sat where he was. He just sat and looked annoyed.

The goose was too big and clumsy, though. For all his mad dashes, for all his loud noises, he could not get near the rat—he only scared the big rat. At last the big boy quieted the goose. That is, he got him to stop his hissing and loud shouting. But the goose was still too excited to be all quiet. Noises just came bubbling up in his throat —fast little excited noises.

In all that noise nobody heard the little old lady at the door. She had rapped and knocked. And knocked some more. She had called the big boy. Nobody had heard anything. Now at last they heard her.

"I've got Tiby here," the little old lady said. "He's all wet and bedraggled from hunting in the swamp. He seems awfully tired."

"Bring him in," the big boy said. "Tiby is never too tired to hunt."

In came Tiby. Bang went the door. For a moment Tiby stood and looked surprised at all the animals and all the mixup in the room. He did not seem able to understand it. But then his little nose went up. Up and up. He sniffed and sniffed. The rat now was very quiet. He had crawled far behind a box. He sat there waiting between the wall and the box.

Tiby walked straight for that box. He stuck his head into the space between the box and the wall. He wasn't even the tiniest bit excited. Not that anybody could see. He didn't swish his tail, he didn't hunch his back, his hair didn't stand up.

He just walked slowly into that space between the box and the wall. He crawled very slowly into that narrow space and at the end of that narrow space, the rat was sitting. Sitting quietly, waiting—waiting for that cat to come on.

Then there was the sound of a scuffle. Nobody could see just what was going on. All that could be seen was the tip of Tiby's bushy tail. Now Tiby was coming out. The space was too narrow for him to turn around; he had to back out slowly. First his tail came into view, then his hind legs.

"He's got the rat," the big boy shouted to the little old lady. "Tiby's got the rat—he's the real cat. He isn't any bigger than the rat, but he isn't afraid."

"Now that's what I call a useful animal," Grandpa said. "A lot more useful than that blundering no-good goose."

But the big boy was wrong. The grandfather was all

wrong. Slowly Tiby came backing out. Every moment there was a little more of him. There he was now. There came the rat. But it wasn't Tiby who had the rat—the rat had Tiby. That rat had hold of the cat.

The big boy's eyes went wide and round. The grandfather chewed nervously on his lip. All the animals were very still. It became very quiet in that room. And then they saw. The rat was hanging on to Tiby. When Tiby had stuck his head into that narrow space the rat had bitten him right in the cheek, right in his long hair. And there he hung.

Was Tiby excited? Was he afraid? Not the least bit. Now he and the rat were in the open. Tiby stood there and quietly raised his head high, then he shook it. The rat hung on. He shook it again. This time the rat had to let go. But before Tiby could grab him, that rat had darted straight back into that narrow space between the wall and the box.

Again and again Tiby tried, but it was just no use. That cat simply did not have enough room in that narrow space to twist his head. Each time the rat bit the cat, instead of the cat biting the rat. It was lucky for Tiby that he had very long hair on his cheeks.

The big boy tried to wrench the box away. He couldn't. It was too heavy.

"Here," Grandpa said. "Try the goose. He's got a long thin neck. He can reach that rat."

"But a goose can't catch a rat," the big boy said. "The rat will bite him."

"Well," Grandpa growled. "He might as well prove himself really useful." And he shoved the goose right up to the box.

Like lightning that goose darted his long slim neck into that narrow space. It didn't even take a moment.

The big boy's eyes almost popped out of his head. Grandpa's mouth stood round with surprise.

The goose had the rat. Had him by the neck. There hung the rat limp and helpless.

"Open the door, Mother!" the big boy screamed. "Open the door! The goose caught the rat!"

The little old lady opened the door, then she hurried and ran to the other side of the room.

Out came the goose, the big rat dangling high in the air.

Out came Oatmeal Joe, very much excited now and wide awake.

Out came Tiby, very much disappointed he had not caught the rat.

Out came the big boy, telling his mother very loudly just what the big goose had done.

Out came Grandpa, too surprised at that big goose to say even one word.

And last of all, out came the little yellow baby cat, still keeping as far from the big rat as possible—still a wee bit afraid, even though the big goose had the rat.

Then the little old lady came, too. Behind the baby cat. That way she was farthest away from the rat.

It was the queerest procession you ever saw. Everybody excited, everybody talking that could talk. Everybody noisy. All but the big goose. For once that goose was quiet—he could not shout and hold the rat at the same time.

Through the house that procession marched, all

following the big goose. They marched through the kitchen, then through the back door. Out marched the goose into the dark farmyard.

The big boy quickly switched on the electric light that hung in the windmill, so they could watch the finish of the fight. But there was no finish to that fight. For no sooner did the goose have the rat out of the house than he let him go. And none of the cats made a single move to get the rat again. The goose and all the cats and all the people stood in a row watching that rat run away.

The rat ran past the chicken coop, around the big maple tree, and disappeared behind the old, tumbledown shed.

"I'm glad the goose let that rat go," said the little old lady. "He was a brave rat."

"I'm glad too," said the big boy. "That rat put up a brave fight against the cats and the big goose and big me."

But Grandpa was not glad. He looked hard at the little old lady. He looked disgustedly at the big boy.

"Glad, glad!" he sputtered. "Glad that rat got away

to eat all the corn for the chickens? Can you tell me what there is to be glad about that?"

"But you have to admit that goose did catch the rat. Now do you think he was useful?" the big boy asked.

Grandpa muttered something, but nobody heard what he muttered. For just that moment the goose set up a great shout. He had remembered the hole under the storeroom window.

He marched straight up to the window, shouting as he went. The big boy followed him. Grandpa followed him. Then they saw that the bottle had fallen out of the hole. Then they knew how the rat had gotten into the house.

The big boy picked up the bottle. He put it back in the hole. He gave it an extra hard shove. Then he gave it an extra hard kick.

"This is the time the goose really showed you up," that big boy said to Grandpa. "If you had fixed that hole properly, as you said you would, that rat would never have gotten into the house."

The little old lady bit her fingers when she heard the

big boy say that to Grandpa. He shouldn't have said it. Shouldn't have said it.

"Show me up!" Grandpa sputtered. "Show me up! I'll show him. I . . ." Then he became so angry he could not say more.

He could not say a word. He could not even wave his arms. He was so angry, he marched himself straight off to bed without finishing his supper.

He lay in bed muttering to himself. He lay there counting on his fingers how many days it would be till his eighty-eighth birthday.

"Show me up," he muttered over and over again. "I'll show him! Now I certainly won't wait till my eighty-eighth birthday. Even though it's just four days off."

He got up. He dressed himself again. He stole down the stairs. He caught the goose and shoved him into the fattening-box. Then he put in enough corn for ten geese.

The little duck went quite frantic when he was separated from the goose. He ran and ran around the big box until he was too tired even to whisper his quacks to himself.

But the little old lady heard the commotion Grandpa made with the goose. She saw what he had done. She turned quite pale, but she knew it was useless to argue with Grandpa—not when he was in that great rage.

Then she saw the little frantic duck. She took pity on him. She set him in the fattening-crate with the big goose. Then that little duck was happy—then he was contented. But that little old lady had made a great mistake.

For when Grandpa saw the duck in the fattening-crate with the big goose, he chuckled. He chuckled very disagreeably down in his dry old throat. Over and over again.

"Fine," he said. "That's fine. I had never thought of that, but it's very fine. It's a wonderful idea. That roasting pan is big enough for both the goose and the little duck."

And here it was only four days to the grandpa's eighty-eighth birthday. And there sat the goose in the fattening-crate—punished although he had been almost more useful than ever before.

10

The Goose Who Caught a Tramp

THIS was the day the big boy had to bring eggs to town —there was nothing wrong with that.

But this was the day that the farmer from the next-door farm had come to tell the big boy and his mother that there was a tramp in the neighborhood—there was plenty wrong with that.

And this was the day it was Grandpa's eighty-eighth birthday. And that was terrible.

"I don't like to leave you here alone," the big boy told his mother. "Not with that big tramp in the neighborhood."

He fussed and fretted quite a bit about that tramp because the more he thought about the tramp the less he would have to think about the big goose on this eighty-eighth birthday of Grandpa's.

"Nonsense," the little old lady told the big boy quite sharply, "You'd better go. I'm not afraid of tramps. Why should I be afraid of tramps with Grandpa and a big shepherd dog to protect me?"

Other times she would have said, "With that big goose to protect me." But she did not say it now. She did not dare say it. That goose was still in the fattening-crate. He could not protect anybody. It would have made her too sad even to mention the goose. In fact, she felt so sad she wanted to be alone. That was why she told the big boy to go deliver his eggs. That was why she spoke to him quite sharply.

But the big boy was not satisfied. He still was very worried. First he went back of the barn and whistled for Sam, the big shepherd dog.

At last, after he had whistled at least five times, Sam came bounding out of the pasture.

"Now you stay here," the big boy told him. "And don't you dare go out of the yard. Never mind your sparrows. You can chase those some other day."

Sam, the big shepherd dog, didn't like that a bit. Ever since the goose had come to the farm he had been free to chase sparrows and rabbits and dig for woodchucks. He had not caught a single one yet, but that didn't bother Sam one bit—it was a lot of fun chasing them anyway. Why, he had gone right on doing it these last four days, although the goose was locked up in the fattening-crate and could not guard the yard.

But he had to stay in the yard this morning, like it or not. For, after all, the big boy had ordered him to guard the yard.

Next the big boy went to hunt up the grandfather. He was working at the old, tumbledown shed. He had taken a long board and laid it on a slant from the ground to the edge of the shed roof. Then he had tied a rope around that board as high as he could reach. He left one end of that rope dangling loose.

"Look," he said to the big boy. "That's where I'll hang the goose to dress him. But first I'm going way back in the field, back of the pond to pick some beans and maybe I'll even find a summer squash that's big enough. I wanted cranberry sauce and pumpkin pie with my roast goose, but I guess beans and squash will have to do."

The big boy did not want to listen to that.

"Look here, Grandpa," he said. "There's a tramp in the neighborhood. You'd better not go way back of the pond—that's too far from the house. You'd better stay here and take care of Mother."

"Not go to the fields," Grandpa spluttered. "Not go to the fields and pick beans and hunt squash! What's the matter with you? Can you tell me that? Are you afraid of an old tramp? I'll take my hoe along. I'll hit him over the head when he comes. I'm going to the field; I'm going right now. First I'll pick beans, then I'll hunt squash, and then I'll fix the goose."

And off he marched. But he had hardly taken twenty steps when back he marched.

"Here," he said, "here's a quarter for cranberries."

"But cranberries are out of season."

"Take it, anyway. And you see that you get some cranberries. It's bad enough I have to go without pumpkin pie with my roast goose. Yes, and roast duck."

The big boy waited until the grandfather was out of sight. Then he went to the fattening-crate. He opened it. He took the big goose out. He even took the little duck out.

Neither the big boy nor the little old lady had dared to let that big goose out of the fattening-crate before. But now the big boy was desperate with worry over the big tramp in the neighborhood.

He said to himself: "If Grandpa won't stay here to protect my mother, then the big goose will have to do it. He will love to do it. Maybe Grandpa won't mind so much that the big goose is free a little while on his eighty-eighth birthday."

And he said to the goose: "Goosie, you'd better keep your sharp eyes peeled for that tramp. You can see a mile, so keep a sharp lookout. But you'd better not shout very loud because then Grandpa might hear. And then . . ."

He did not finish. He hurried to his little truck. He jumped in and rushed away. He quite forgot his new yellow bucket with eggs, he was so worried. The little old lady forgot about those eggs, too, she was so sad.

But the big goose marched straight to the front yard. He kept very quiet.

The big boy needn't have told that goose to keep watch. That is what he did every day without being told—just because he loved it. He had done that every single day since coming to the farm, except for the time he ran away. And except for the four days he had sat in the fattening-crate.

The big boy rushed down the road. He drove very fast, because the faster he went, the sooner he would be back.

Then as he drove over the little bridge across the creek under the road, the big boy thought he saw a bundle of clothes on the bank of that creek. But he was going so fast, he could not be very sure. "No," he decided, "it's only an old black piece of tar paper that blew off somebody's barn.

If the big boy had only stopped to look—he would have caught the tramp right then and there. For that was no tar paper he saw on the bank of that creek. It was a bundle of clothes, and inside of those clothes was the tramp—fast asleep.

But the boy did not stop. He drove straight on in the greatest hurry to get to town.

And just after the big boy had rattled over that bridge, the tramp woke up. He sat up and stretched.

"I'm hungry," said the tramp, stretching himself. "I'm going to some farmhouse to get something to eat."

But first he took a needle and thread out of one coat pocket. Then a very bright red rag out of another pocket. And then he started to sew that bright red rag on the back of his brown coat. With great big stitches of white thread.

After that, he set out to get some food. And the very first house he would come to was the one where the little old lady was all alone.

But the big goose spied him long before he got near the house. The minute that tramp came around the bend in the road, the big goose saw him. And such a racket as that goose set up. He quite forgot about the big boy's warning to keep quiet. He set up such a racket you could hear him all over the countryside. It was a wonder Grandpa did not hear him. But Grandfather was so far from the house, and he was stooped so low to the ground searching for squash, he never heard that goose.

The tramp heard it. And he stopped still in the middle of the road. Then he made believe he was going back. He walked until he was around the bend of the road again. After that he ducked very low and walked around the hill, then through the woods, then through the cornfield straight for the little pond on the other side of the cornfield.

And there Grandpa was. On his hands and knees. Picking beans, hunting for squash. On came the tramp straight for Grandpa. Then Grandpa rose to his feet. He grasped his hoe. He held it high above his head. He rushed for the big tramp.

"Off my land!" he screamed. "Off my land right this minute!" First his face went white, then it went red, then it went purple.

But that big tramp did not move an inch. He just stood there on the edge of the cornfield and folded his big arms across his great chest. He laughed and laughed.

On came the grandfather. He swung his hoe. Then all of a sudden that tramp moved. First he grabbed the hoe. Away it went, clear over the pond, clear over the fallen-down willow at the end of the pond.

Then he grabbed Grandpa. Way in the air, way above his head he held him. There was Grandpa, squirming and kicking and biting high up in the air. That big tramp just held him there and laughed and laughed.

"Let me down this minute!" squealed Grandpa. "This minute, I tell you!"

"All right, I'll let you down," laughed the tramp.

And he took Grandpa and threw him into the pond. There he landed with a great splash. On hands and knees. In the middle of the pond. Grandpa scrambled erect. He pulled his hands out of the mud. He tried to pull his legs out of the mud. First he pulled on the right leg, then he pulled on the left leg. But when he pulled on the right leg, his left leg sank deeper in the mud; and when he pulled on the left leg, his right leg sank deeper in the mud.

There stood Grandpa in the middle of the pond. Struggling and struggling, and the more he struggled the deeper he sank into the mud. Now he was up to his knees in the mud.

He screamed at the tramp. He tried to scold him the way he sometimes did the big boy and the little old lady. And the way he always scolded the big goose.

But the tramp only laughed. He took the pan of beans and threw them into the pond with Grandpa. He took the one green summer squash Grandpa had found and kicked it all to pieces. Kicked it into the pond.

There Grandpa stood in the middle of the pond struggling; there he stood with his red stocking cap askew. And an empty pan and hundreds of beans and little pieces of summer squash floating all around him. There he stood calling for help, but he had gone too far from home for anybody to hear his hoarse, old voice. Only the tramp heard him.

And the tramp walked on to the house.

The big goose did not see him. He was in the front yard looking down the road to see if the tramp would come back. That goose had stood there so long the little white duck had gotten tired of standing there with him. He had gone off and found himself a nice mud puddle behind the tank for the cows.

Sam, the big shepherd dog, did not see him. Sam was lying back of the chicken coop in a patch of sun, fast asleep. Every now and then he twitched his feet and wiggled his ears—he was dreaming of chasing sparrows in the pasture.

The tramp knocked on the door.

At last the little old lady came.

She opened the door just a slit. Then she saw the tramp. She tried to slam the door shut again, but she was just too late. She couldn't close the door. That tramp had stuck his foot between it and the doorpost.

"What do you want?" said the little old lady.

"I want food."

"No," said the little old lady. "Not now."

"And I want a new coat," said the tramp.

"No," said the little old lady. "Not now."

"Why not now?"

"Because my son is away. He went to town."

And that was where the little old lady made a very bad mistake. For now the tramp knew she was home all alone.

"I want to come in," he said.

"You can't," said the little old lady. "Not now."

"I can't?" said the tramp. "I can't? I'll show you."

And he started pushing the door very hard. The little old lady could never hold that door.

"Goosie, Goosie, Goosie!" she screamed.

"I'm not afraid of any goose," the tramp said with a laugh.

"Here, Sam! Here, Sam!" screamed the old lady.

"And I'm not afraid of any dog," said the tramp.

"Grandpa, Grandpa!" screamed that little old lady.

"Hah," laughed the tramp. "Ha, ha, ha. I don't think Grandpa *can* come."

And then he stopped laughing. For the moment the little lady had opened her mouth that big goose had come. He actually flew, he came so fast. He was at least two feet from the ground. Around the house he came, straight for that tramp.

And now the dog was awake, too. The tramp ran toward the chicken coop with the goose close behind him. And the big shepherd dog stood up. There was that tramp between that big goose and that big dog. It looked as if things were going badly with him. He couldn't go ahead, and he couldn't go back.

At last he managed to jump clear over the tank for the cows. He jumped so hard that he even jumped over the puddle behind the tank in which the little duck was playing. He landed with a thud. But that little duck had his head so deep in the mud he never saw the tramp. He never even heard that tramp land on both his big, flat feet right beside his puddle.

But that high clumsy jump didn't help the big tramp, for the minute the tramp ran down the driveway the goose was after him, and the dog circled around him. The goose caught him. Right by the back of his flying coat. He caught hold of that red patch the tramp had sewed on that very morning. And he ripped it right off.

It was lucky for that tramp he had sewed that red

rag on his coat with such big stitches or the goose would surely have had him. It was even luckier for that tramp that right at that moment the big boy drove into the yard. You see the boy had missed his bucket of eggs and had come right back. If he hadn't come just at that moment Sam would have had the tramp right then and there.

"Call off that goose; call off that dog, mister," screamed the tramp.

The big boy jumped out of his truck and called off the dog. It wasn't so easy to call off the goose though. He was angry through and through by this time, and he was bound to do things to that tramp. In fact, it wasn't until they called the little old lady, and she took the goose in her arms, that he would let the tramp alone.

"And now get out of here just as fast as you can," said the big boy to the tramp.

"But I'm so hungry, mister," said the tramp. But first he looked out of the corner of his eye at the goose and then out of the corner of his other eye at the dog. He was still afraid.

"Maybe I had better go in the house and get him some bread," the little old lady said. She felt a little bit sorry for that tramp, too, in spite of what he had done. That was the way that little old lady was—she was almost too kind.

"But then you must first promise never to come back here again," the big boy told the tramp in a very hard voice.

"Don't worry, mister. I'll never come back. Not with that goose and that dog." And once more the tramp looked out of the corner of his eye first at the dog and then at the goose. He kept his eye on that goose, for now the little old lady had gone into the house to get him some bread, and the goose was standing very close to the tramp.

"And please, mister, I need a new coat," said the tramp. "I fixed this one all up this morning. And that big goose tore it all to pieces."

He looked at the back of his coat, and he saw the red rag was gone. Then that big tramp started to cry.

The big boy had to laugh. "And if I give you another coat will you promise . . .?"

The big boy did not have to finish.

"Don't worry, mister, I'll never come back. Not with that big goose and that big dog."

Then the little old lady came out with three slices of bread and an old coat of the big boy's.

Then the tramp went—the new coat in one hand and the three slices of bread in the other hand.

And he bit from all three slices at once.

There he went. He would take a few steps. Then look around to see if that goose were coming. Then he'd quickly take a bite from all three slices of bread.

But when the big boy went into the house, and the big goose and the dog were by themselves in the yard, that tramp just turned around once. And when he saw the two of them there, he didn't take another bite. He started to run as fast as he could. Faster and faster. And the last that big goose saw of that tramp, he was still running as he disappeared over a hill.

But the goose was not sure. Maybe, he thought, that tramp will do just the way he did this morning and

circle back again. He flew to the highest part of the yard
near the windmill. But from there he could not see over
the hill.

That goose looked all around for a higher place.
If only he could fly up on the chicken coop. But he could
never fly that high. At best he could only fly two feet
off the ground, because he was that heavy. Then he saw
the long plank. He saw that long plank Grandpa had
put on a slant from the ground to the edge of the roof
of the tumbledown shed.

The goose did not hesitate a moment. He spread
his wings. He almost flew toward that plank. Ran a little,
flew a little. Straight up the plank he sailed. There he
was on the edge of the roof.

He saw the tramp. He saw he was still running. But
what was that he saw just out of the corner of his eye?
He turned to get a better look. Yes, it was Grandpa's red
stocking cap. He could just see it with his keen eyes over
the leaves of the fallen-down willow on the edge of the
pond.

That was all wrong. Ducks and geese went swimming in ponds, but grandpas never went in ponds.

That goose rushed along the edge of the roof. He sailed right off that roof. Then he ran and he flew, he flew and he ran in the greatest hurry to get to that pond.

Soon he was there. There was Grandpa still standing exactly where he had landed in the middle of the pond.

The goose did not know what to make of it. He swam out to Grandpa, he swam in big circles around Grandpa. Then in little circles, then closer and closer to Grandpa.

And all the time he made deep surprised clucking noises down in his soft throat. He could not understand why Grandpa wanted to stand in the middle of that pond.

But Grandpa became very angry.

"Why don't you shout for help now?" he shouted. "You can make enough unnecessary noise otherwise. But when you've got to help me . . ."

But the goose kept right on swimming very close to the grandfather's legs. He kept right on making those surprised clucking noises down in his throat.

It sounded to the grandfather as if the goose were laughing at him. It sounded as if that goose were chuckling deep down in his throat.

Grandpa's face went white, then red, then purple. Then it went pale again—and it stayed pale.

"If you've come out here to laugh at me—the way that big tramp did, then . . . then I'll duck you under!" he roared.

He grabbed the goose. He grabbed him by the neck with one hand. And with the other hand he pressed down on the goose's back.

But he could press all he wanted, he could not push that goose underwater. He could push him down until all but his head was under water, but that was as far as he could get the goose down. Then that goose would just swim all the harder. He would paddle his feet at a furious pace and keep himself above water. That goose was too strong; he was too good a swimmer to be ducked.

Then Grandpa discovered a strange thing. A very wonderful thing. He found that when he pressed down on the goose, he could pull one leg free from the mud.

That is what he did. First he pulled his right leg free. Then he took a great big step. Then, still holding on to the goose, he pulled his left leg free. Then he took another big step. In that way, in five big steps with his right leg, and five big steps with his left leg, Grandpa walked to the edge of the pond.

Then he climbed out. The goose climbed out. He set up a great shout. He shouted and shouted and shouted.

This time Grandpa did not scold him for making too much noise. That grandfather did not bother to pick up his hoe. He did not bother to fish out the pan and the beans that had floated to the edge of the pond. He did not bother with any of those things.

No, he picked up the big goose. Wet as he was. He picked up the big goose right in his arms the way the little old lady did it, and the way the big boy did it. He picked him up in his arms and he hugged him tight.

That had never happened before. But the big goose understood. He chuckled deep down in his soft throat, he nibbled at Grandpa's face. He nipped at Grandpa's ear. He even ran his big bill through Grandpa's hair, and he pushed his red stocking cap off. It fell on the ground. The grandfather did not even bother to pick it up. He marched straight for the house with the goose in his arms.

The little old lady and the big boy had heard the goose's shouts. They had come out of the house. There they saw Grandpa coming with the goose.

"Oh, oh!" said the big boy. "Here comes Grandpa with the goose. Do you suppose if we tell him about the tramp . . ."

"But look!" the little old lady interrupted him. "Look! Grandpa is carrying the goose in his arms. Do you suppose . . . ?"

They did not know what to think. They hardly dared to think. They both just stood right where they were and watched Grandpa coming toward them with the goose in his arms.

But the grandfather did not come right to them. First he went into the big barn. He went into the horse stable. And when he came out of the barn he wasn't carrying the goose in his arms any more. He held the goose under one arm. And he held the big roasting pan under the other arm.

"Oh, oh!" said the big boy, and his voice was very husky.

"Oh, oh!" said the old lady, and her voice trembled very much.

But even then the grandfather did not come right to them. First he went to the tank for the cows. There he set down the goose. Then he took the big roasting pan and filled it with water from the tank for the cows.

He walked with that big roasting pan right past the little old lady and the big boy. He did not say a word. He could not. That roasting pan full of water was so heavy he could not talk. All he could do was grunt.

He set the roasting pan right next to the dishpan in which the goose always took his bath. He picked up the dishpan and threw it over the fence.

"It seems to me," he grumbled, "if you want to keep a goose—you should keep him proper. How could that goose sit in that little dishpan?"

The little old lady and the big boy looked and looked. They heard the grandfather grumble, but they also saw him smile.

"Do you mean . . . ?" asked the big boy.

"Do you mean . . . ?" asked the little old lady.

Then they both asked it right together. "Do you mean that big goose can stay on this farm forever?"

"Of course, he can," Grandpa shouted. "Of course, he can! What do you think? Can you tell me that? Do you think I want to eat such a useful goose on my eighty-eighth birthday? Or on my eighty-ninth birthday? Or even on my hundredth birthday? Can you . . ."

But he could not finish. He had to laugh too hard. The boy and the old lady laughed too. But the grandfather laughed the hardest of all. He laughed so hard that even the little duck, who had his head under the mud of his puddle near the tank for the cows, heard him. He lifted his head out of the mud. He came running.

But he came just a bit too late. He tried to run to the big goose, but he was too late. For now the big goose was really excited.

He called and he called, shouted and shouted. He called so loudly the grandfather could hardly tell the little old lady about how the goose had rescued him. He shouted so loudly the little old lady could hardly tell the grandfather about how the goose had saved her from the tramp.

He called and he shouted. He ran and he flew. Ran a little, flew a little. Faster and faster. Around and around the house. He flew to the big boy, he flew to the grandfather.

That little duck could never follow the goose that fast. He tried, but it was just no use. So he sat down at the little old lady's feet. And in that the little white duck did quite right.

For last of all that big goose flew to the little old lady. He stood there next to the little duck and stretched his long neck higher than ever before. He shouted louder and longer. Again and again. And this is what the big goose seemed to shout: "I am glad I saved my little old lady from the tramp. And I am glad I helped Grandpa out of the pond. I am terribly glad, for now I can stay on the farm forever. On this farm I love. With the little old lady and the little white duck. With the big boy who brought me here. And with Grandpa who is a fine fellow after all. With the cows and calves and Molly the horse. With Oatmeal Joe and all the other cats. With the freckled cow. And the funny baby bull. With the little football pig. And even with Sam the big shepherd, who chases sparrows—as if he could ever catch a sparrow!"

That is what the big goose tried to shout. And that was why he was so happy.

And that is what the little duck tried to shout. Every word of it exactly after the big goose. And he too tried to shout louder than he ever had before in all his life. At the top of his voice!

But for all that, nobody could hear that little duck. His little bill opened and shut, opened and shut—faster and faster. Still nobody could hear him—even if the big goose had not shouted at all. Nobody could hear that little whisper.

But the big goose shouted on. On and on. Louder and louder. About Tiby, the hunter cat. About Topsy, the old white horse. About the black cow who had *not* stepped on Grandpa.

He shouted about everything on that farm. Every little thing he could remember. He even shouted about the big rat who had come into the house—although that rat had long ago left the farm.

At last he could remember nothing more to shout

about. So he started all over from the beginning. But he did not get very far—his big bill was getting too tired.

He got as far as: "On the farm forever."

Then he stopped—he could get no further. He did not even try.

For now he knew *that* was exactly why he was so happy.

He knew!

And it made him so happy all over again that, tired as his big bill was, he had to shout it once more.

So he stretched his long neck. He spread his great wings. He puffed out his downy white chest. He opened his bill to its widest.

Then that shout came. Louder than loud! "ON THE FARM FOREVER!"